MW01517233

The Missing Thane's War

The Four Kingdoms Saga: Book II

Brandon Draga

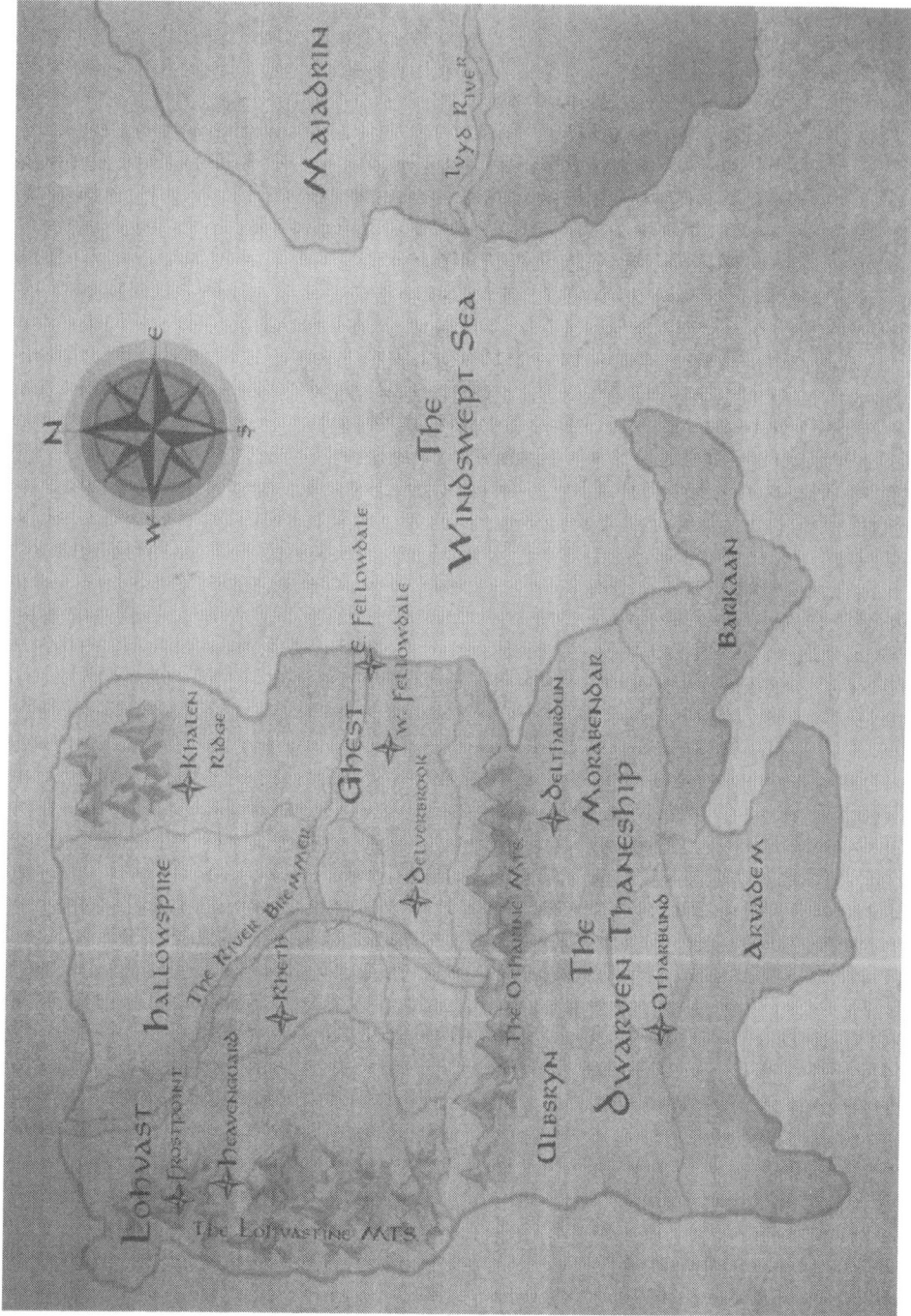

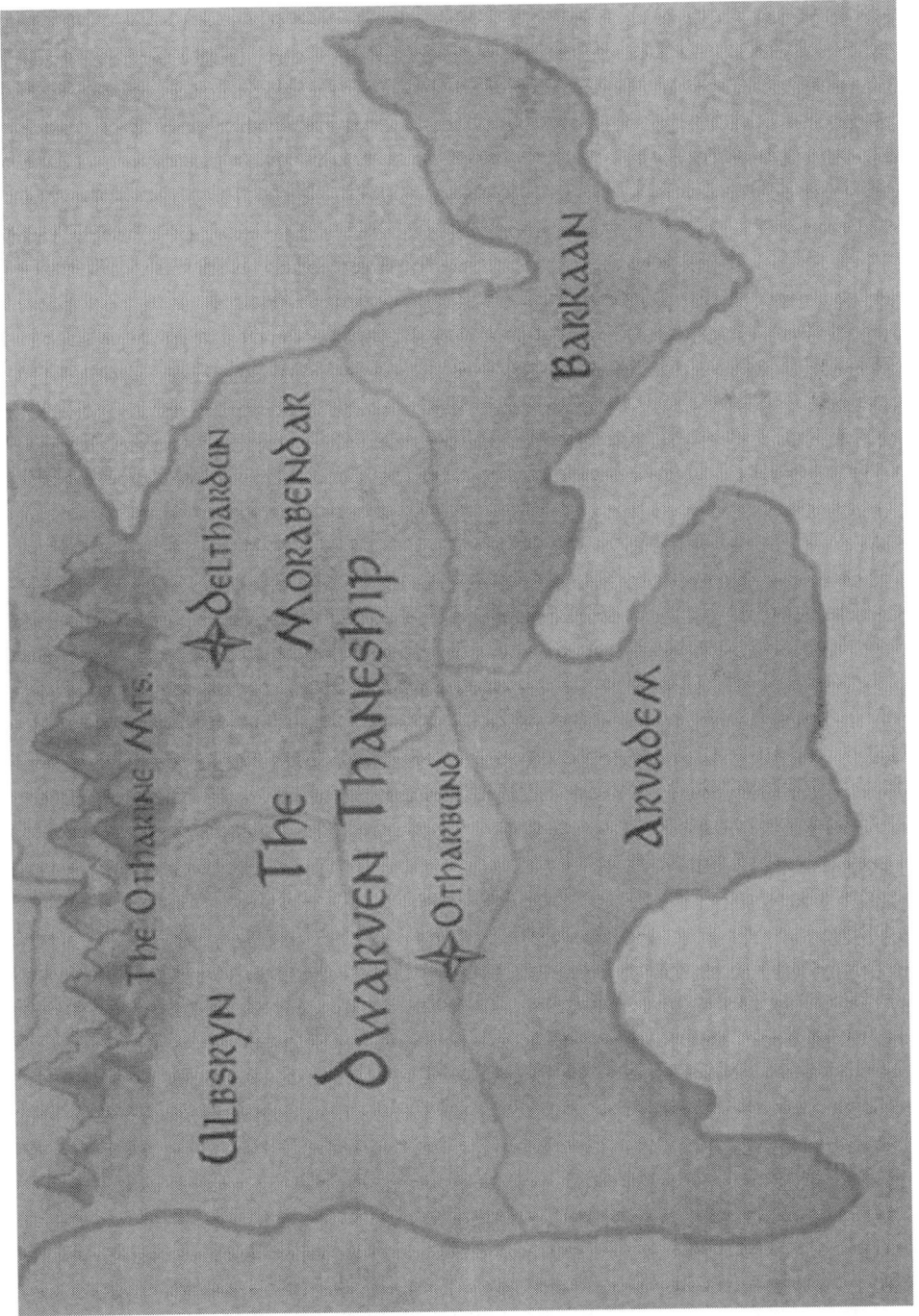

Brandon Draga

OTHER BOOKS BY BRANDON DRAGA

The Four Kingdoms Saga
Book I: *The Summerlark Elf*

Other Works
Dragon in the Doghouse (with *Deanna Laver*)

PRAISE FOR *The Summerlark Elf*

"...Draga likes to mess with traditional stuff like Orcs and wizards and black conspiracies, but he has just enough creativity to make it his own."
- Caleb Hill, Acerbic Writing

"3 out of 4 stars...a light read for anyone who loves fantasy and can't get enough of it."
- Norma Rudolph, Online Book Club

"...Draga does a stellar job of mixing likeable characters with shady scoundrels that become unlikely heroes... I cannot wait for the second book."
- Stephen Fisher, Readers' Favorite

Brandon Draga

Acknowledgments

If you had told me eighteen months ago that I had it in me to write a novel, I would have scoffed. Had you told me I would write two in the span of one year, I'd have questioned your sanity. Had you suggested that I would have the greatest people in the world to help and support me along the way, however, I would not have batted an eyelash. Listed below are but a handful of the friends and family that make up my amazing support system, without whom I would be lost, and the Four Kingdoms nonexistent.

To my wonderful beta readers/pro-bono editors, your advice helped make each draft better than the last, and your enthusiasm helped me want to give you only the best I could offer.

To Jason, who has been as great a friend and a mentor as one could ask for, you have provided advice and opportunities that I could not have fathomed, and have been instrumental in helping me get to where I am today as a creator.

To my family, Mom and Dad, Ryan, Elliott, and Nikki, your love and support have kept me driven, your honesty and guidance have kept me humble and focused, and your pride and belief in me have made me feel like I'm already a bestseller.

Lastly, to Deanna, you have been a patient ear during my moments of self-assurance, a voice of reason during my moments of self-doubt, and a skillful hand who has helped colour this world inside my head. Much of the Four Kingdoms is as much yours as it is mine.

Brandon Draga

The Missing Thane's War

The Missing Thane's War

Prologue

The streets of East Fellowdale were abustle. Merchants hollered boisterously from their carts and storefronts, each one trying to propel his or her voice above the din of the streets so as to whisk patrons away from the competition. Burly sailors littered the docks along the city's coastal border, most of whom were either joyously celebrating their impending departure to parts unknown and the inevitable adventure that accompanied, or wearily thanking the Gods for some much-needed shore leave. Some brought with them wares to sell, while others carried full purses and were anxious to buy. Many were perusing the goods being offered by a number of less-than-scrupulous ladies of varying races, whose marketing tactics were similar to the merchants', though raucous voices were instead replaced by racy clothing. Amid the organized chaos, Professor Falken Coldstone walked with short, but determined steps, paying no mind to any of what was going on around him. The professor had walked the streets of East Fellowdale for so much of his life that he was used to the barrage of sights and sounds that accompanied them. This is not to say that the professor was any less attracted to fancy trinkets and doe-eyed women than most other men, but rather that he was able to tune such things out when something emerged that spoke to his inexhaustible desire for knowledge. Coldstone beamed as he strode toward his manor several blocks away, knowing just such a thing had come his way.

The professor thought back to the meeting he had not an hour earlier. It had begun as an average enough visit to see Caliope Hollowpot, head priestess to the local temple of Bremmer. Coldstone and the old halfling had been good friends for years, and the two typically met weekly, sharing lunch and speaking as old friends do. Caliope was always quick to lend an ear for the professor to fill with talk of his latest studies, and conversely he was happy to afford the priestess a captive audience to whom she could regale the local news and gossip. On this particular occasion, the pair had sat at a small table in the taproom of the Merchant's Quilt, one of the more reputable dockside inns.

"There's word Miss Sanella Sweetwater is looking for a new patron," Caliope began, sipping a spoonful of soup daintily.

"Oh?" the professor looked up from his own meal. While he was not particularly interested in the local arts, he remained attentive to his friend.

"It's the truth," Caliope nodded. "Word is she was doing quite well out on the borders of Hallowspire, what with Lord Elkhevian paying her way, but the good Lord had to up and leave for Rheth, something about an attempted coup while his sister was at court there."

"Intriguing." The professor's response was less placating then the last. An attempted coup in Hallowspire's capital? This was a far cry from the banality Caliope usually spoke about.

"Isn't it just, though?" she responded. "It was almost three days the poor girl waited before she turned back east, tail between her legs." The halfling took another sip of soup. "Old Anders said he had heard that she was due back in town within the next night or two, likely wanting to have another go at convincing Lord Graylock that her paintings were worth his time and his coin."

Coldstone peered thoughtfully at his own meal. "Perhaps I should have a word with the girl."

"Professor Coldstone!" Caliope's voice was one of sing-songy surprise. "I had no idea you had any interest in being a patron of the arts. You're always going on about your studies, I always assumed you preferred words to paint." She stopped a moment, and raised one eyebrow suggestively. "Unless it isn't young Miss Sweetwater's paintings you're after?"

Coldstone nonchalantly waved the accusations away. "Oh, come now, Caliope," he admonished, "I only wish to see if she had any more information about that coup in Rheth you mentioned. Unless there's anything else you know of it?"

"Oh," the halfling said, seemingly a bit deflated. "No, I can't say I do. The Gods only know if Sanella would have heard anything. You know how those Midwesterners are, all secretive. Such a queer bunch." Caliope paused a moment then, looking as if something had jogged her memory. "Now that you mention it, though, I know someone who might know something."

"Hm?" Coldstone asked, perking up like a fox that just caught a scent. He had a feeling the old halfling might have been holding out on him.

Caliope chuckled at her old friend's visible excitement. "Quite, Professor." She motioned him close toward her and proceeded with little more than a hoarse whisper. "I received word from an old friend about one week ago that he and three others were en route here from Rheth. Apparently one is an elf from the area who's looking to learn as much as she can about the fae-folk."

Coldstone's eyes widened. "What?!" he gasped, trying his best to maintain a whisper himself. "An elf from Hallowspire? How is that even possible?"

"Your guess is as good as my own," the halfling responded. "All I know is that my knowledge of fae-folk pales in comparison to your own, and when my friend and his companions arrive, I would be more than happy to send them your way. You could give this elf the information she is looking for, and maybe she could tell you more about this coup of yours."

The Professor broke the huddle, nodding thoughtfully as he leaned back into his seat. "That isn't a bad idea." He said as he stood up from the table. "Lunch is my treat this week. Do let me know when your friend arrives."

"I'll be sure to," Caliope responded as she stood up. The professor paid the barkeep, and the two exited together.

"There's something I don't quite understand, Caliope," Coldstone looked down at the halfling as they walked out into a brisk late autumn day. "You said you heard from this friend of yours a week ago, how am I only just hearing of it now?"

"Oh hush!" Caliope playfully smacked the Professor on the arm. "I may be an old gossip, but this individual is a close, personal friend." She looked at Coldstone knowingly, "and you of all people, Professor Coldstone, ought to know that I take the business of my close friends very seriously."

By the time he had finished recollecting the conversation, the Professor had arrived at the doorstep of his home, a fairly large house situated near the heart of East Fellowdale, boasting two levels and a well-kept property line. Coldstone then proceeded to enter the abode, the inside of which was in stark contrast to the outside. Nearly every foreseeable wall from the home's threshold all the way to the kitchen at the opposite end was lined with bookshelves, and each of those bookshelves was lined with books. That is not to say that the books on the shelves were organized, as little could have been further from the truth. Books sat next to one another in such a way that, to anyone but the Professor, would seemingly have no business even taking up shelf space in the same room. What's more was the fact that Professor Coldstone's collection was apparently so vast and varied, containing not only books, but countless maps and scrolls as well. The furniture and floors were nearly as littered with parchment as the walls were. The Professor moved through one of the scant, narrow pathways on the floor without a second thought, traversing the chaos into what could only be recognized as a study if pointed out by Coldstone himself.

The Professor walked over to the bookshelf opposite of the study's entrance, methodically scanning the numerous leather spines before pointing out a particular title with several elven letters written in goldleaf. He pulled the book from the shelf and began to carefully thumb through it as he made his way to his nearby desk. The Professor propped the book open and upright on a pile of closed books on the left side of the desk and held it open with his left hand as his right flipped open a smaller book in the centre of the desk. He took a quill from a nearby inkwell, and began to write.

17 Wenn, AK 388

Strange tidings afoot today, not only in East Fellowdale, but elsewhere. I do not wish to engage in presupposition, but the news I received today from Caliope may be a part of something of incredible consequence, so much so that it could have ripples felt throughout the Four Kingdoms...

Chapter 1

The wheels of Adrik Thornmallet's cart creaked rhythmically as they rolled across the main trade road of the midwestern stretch of Ghest. The dwarf and his companions had been traveling for the past two weeks, and the weather on the road had been temperate enough for the four days since leaving the small town of Troutford that the group had pushed forward relentlessly, stopping only to make camp for the night. The four were exhausted and road-weary, but were anxious enough to reach their destination that they were willing to ignore their fatigue.

Sitting next to Adrik was O'doc Overhill. The halfling smuggler was talking easily with the dwarf, helping to keep morale high, and taking the reins on the cart when Adrik began to tire. O'doc was such a picture of composure that no one was able to notice that he hid an intense worry in his eyes, or that he would look back over his shoulder every so often, certain that they had not seen the last of Lannister Ravenclaw.

In back of the cart lay the halfling's partner, the half-elf Erasmus Stonehand. The bard offered to watch the rear of the cart for trouble, but in his typical nonchalance Erasmus was content to fiddle away on his mandolin, only occasionally glancing outward to the road behind them. More often than not, Erasmus was satisfied with whatever jobs could most easily line his purse, and he and O'doc's time recently spent in Hallowspire certainly did so, albeit through different means than the pair expected. His current trek on the road now, however, had no foreseeable monetary gains attached to it. The bard began to nod off as he contemplated his true reasoning behind going on the journey to the easternmost point of Ghest, when he was startled into full alertness by the end of a small, ornate club nudging him.

The club was held by Enna Summerlark, who looked at Erasmus incredulously and nodded toward the road behind them, indicating that she had been aware of the half-elf's lack of diligence in his task. Erasmus shot the elf a dirty look and proceeded to sit up straight, so as to remain alert. Enna smirked, shook her head, and returned to the large leather-bound book she had been reading for the better part of the day. For Enna, each day on the road had been another day spent reading. Her knowledge of elvish had improved noticeably as a result of this, and by consequence so had her knowledge of arcana. The elf was slightly disheartened, however, for in spite of having spent the better part of three weeks reading through the numerous texts left to her by the former Archmage Varis, she was unable to find any real, concrete information about the Fae Realm, 'the

Kingdom of Wood,' as Varis had called it. Enna's human parents had told her all they could about her birth mother, which was next to nothing, and Enna knew the only way she would get any real answers about her biological parents, or her elven heritage in general, would be to find out more about the Fae Realm. The only problem was, as Varis had shown she and Erasmus back in Rheth, the elves were fiercely protective, and kept almost all knowledge of their people closely guarded. Enna was an elf, yes, but she was an elf raised by humans, and traveling with a dwarf, a halfling, and a half-elf. Her mind tried to think of reasons why any elf would trust her with the secrets of their people, but she was unable to think of a single one.

Enna was shaken from her thoughts as she heard the bray of Adrik's mules and felt the cart come to a stop. Both she and Erasmus looked at one another concernedly, and stepped out the small doors on either side of the cart to investigate. The cart had stopped at a more heavily wooded stretch of the trade road. The canopy of trees, largely bare due to the encroaching winter, cast a latticed shadow across the ground. O'doc sat holding the mules' reins as Adrik crouched down several feet ahead, his hand and eyes to the ground. Enna went to call out to the dwarf, but Erasmus raised a hand to silence her. He walked quietly toward Adrik, beckoning Enna to follow.

"Bandits?" the half-elf whispered to his dwarven companion as he crept closer.

Adrik shook his head. "Would that we should be so lucky," he whispered back. "Observe the miniscule size of these footprints."

Erasmus leaned over Adrik's shoulder and, upon observing the small, crude bootprints, let out an exasperated sigh. "Wonderful," he said. "Goblins."

"Goblins?!" It was everything Enna could do not to cry out. She heard tales of the creatures from merchants who would come through Hallowspire. Vicious, animalistic things that swarmed caravans like locusts, savagely rending beast and man alike, leaving any who survived their attacks horribly diseased.

"More than likely making camp in the woods, hoping to relieve passing merchants of their coin," Adrik responded, the irritated tone of his voice matching that of Erasmus'.

Neither Erasmus nor Adrik seemed to notice Enna standing behind them, her face a portrait of panicked disbelief. The four of them were on the brink of being senselessly eviscerated, and Erasmus and Adrik were crouched down looking at the dirt. "Excuse me," she said, leaning down between the two. "Should we not be trying to get out of here as quickly and quietly as possible, instead of waiting around for goblins to come and rip us to pieces?"

Erasmus looked up at Enna, eyebrow raised, and then back to Adrik, who tried not to chuckle, for fear of embarrassing the young elf. "Milady Enna," the dwarf said, standing up, "I had forgotten that you've not been outside Hallowspire's closely-guarded borders before. I am at a loss to even conceive of what manner of wild stories you've been told of goblins." He placed his hand on Enna's arm comfortingly, "but rest assured, to a quick-witted, well-armed group of travelers such as ourselves, they are little more than foul little nuisances."

Enna relaxed a little, and smiled at the dwarf. Adrik was infinitely more well-traveled than Enna, and she took comfort in his words. The comfort was short lived, however, as the relative silence of the woods was broken by the distinct metallic clang of blades meeting nearby. Enna, Erasmus, and Adrik wheeled around at the noise, which came from the direction of the cart, and ran towards it, weapons in hand.

As the three neared the cart, the source of the noise was made apparent. O'doc, daggers in either hand, was in the midst of fighting off two small, gaunt humanoids with leathery, yellow-orange skin, the hue of which was not dissimilar to the autumn foliage. Each of the goblins held short swords that showed evidence of overuse and under-maintenance, and both were brandishing their notched, rusty weapons at the halfling as they flanked him.

Adrik began to move to the halfling's aid, but Erasmus put a hand to the dwarf's chest. "Don't worry," he said, his eyes affixed to the standoff. "He knows what he's doing."

Both goblins darted toward O'doc from opposite ends, screeching as they raised their swords. O'doc, moving in a way that bordered on instinct, flicked his wrist and sent one of his daggers spinning through the air briefly, finding purchase just below one of the goblins' collarbone. The goblin yelped in pain and fell to its knees, dropping its weapon and grasping at the embedded blade. The sight shocked the second goblin, keeping its attention long enough for it to drop its guard, giving O'doc just enough opportunity to charge, knock it into the ground, and bury his second dagger into its chest. The goblin underneath O'doc struggled briefly before it went limp, and when the halfling was sure it was dead, he removed his dagger and turned around to the first goblin, who was now beginning to stand, albeit with one arm clearly lame from the initial dagger wound. O'doc ran toward the goblin, maneuvering easily around its wild one-armed swing, and driving his dagger deep into its back, causing it to gasp and sputter before it, too, went limp.

The halfling's companions walked toward the scene as he methodically removed his blades from the fallen goblin and cleaned them off with a handkerchief. "That took longer than I expected," Erasmus commented.

"I was aiming for this one's neck, and I missed," Od'oc added belatedly. "Suppose I'm out of practice with my throwing."

"Might there be more of these creatures lurking about?" Adrik asked.

"It's not often goblins travel in pairs." O'doc said, daggers now sheathed as he began to walk back toward the wagon. "I'm sure no one's opposed to passing back into open farmland as quickly as possible." He stopped beside Enna, looking up to see her staring agape at him.

"You just... killed them." she stammered.

"I did, and if I hadn't then they'd have done the same to us," he replied matter-of-factly. "You're lucky that you've seen little yet in life, Enna. You aren't yet bitter. Know this, though, the road can be a dangerous place, and you need to be alright with spilling some blood, because sometimes you'll have to to make sure that blood isn't yours."

The companions regrouped and set back out, with Adrik opting to take a fork in the road. Although this added extra time to their travels, it put the cart back out into the open, away from the possibility of further goblin attacks. The four were tense for some time thereafter, even with Erasmus shedding his usual relaxed demeanor as he kept watch of the cart's rear. Enna spent the better part of the rest of the day's travel deep in thought. O'doc's words had struck her in a very real way. She had, at first, wanted to argue with what the halfling had said, but realized quickly that he was right. He, Erasmus, and Adrik were infinitely more well-versed in the ways of the road than she was, and seemed much more prepared to deal with dangers that, for the first time in Enna's life, were no longer the bedtime stories her father used to tell her. The elf decided that she would not allow herself to be helpless.

Later that day, after the group made camp for the night, Enna walked back to Adrik's cart and found one of Varis' books to read. The book was similar to many of the others: large, leather-bound, and slightly musty smelling. The inside of the book, however, was very different from any of the others Enna had read so far. The pages of this book contained no grand histories, but were instead filled with diagrams, runes, and phrases written in Elvish. That night, Enna Summerlark sat next to the fire and began to read a book of spells.

Chapter 2

Daylen Cresthill sat at his desk deep in the halls of Lohvast's Arcane University, his thumb and middle finger massaging small circles along his temples. Sitting across from the University's Headmaster was Tavon Elbar, Archmage of Lohvast. While Cresthill could not fairly argue that the slight man in the long purple robes was the source of his frustrations for the last month, Elbar was undoubtedly the vessel by which they were brought to him.

"Please understand, Daylen," the Archmage said sympathetically, "I am making this request at the behest of her Grace."

"You needn't remind me, Tavon," the Headmaster responded, looking up at his old colleague in exasperation. "Every damned time you've come to me in the last month it has been at the Queen's behest. First there was the call for the War Mages, then you came to pluck most of the best arcanists from my faculty, and now I am being told that the queen herself is en route to the University? To what end? By the Gods, Tavon, you've blustered in here nearly once a week with these increasingly outrageous demands, and not once have you given me good reason. I'm starting to believe that Her Grace has finally gone off her..."

"*Dina Telu!*" The Archmage cried out, both stopping the Headmaster from continuing and conjuring in an invisible field around the two, its presence known only to them due to their finely-tuned arcane senses.

"Really, Tavon? A silencing barrier?" the Headmaster questioned. "Have you truly become so paranoid over the years in your position that you believe the Queen to be listening to every word you say?"

"Your words are bordering on treason," the Archmage warned nervously. "Need I remind you that Her Grace attended this very university? She is not short of friends and supporters within these walls, and talk like this could put you in grave danger, regardless of your position." Elbar looked pensively at the Headmaster, waiting for a nod of understanding before waving his hand and dispelling the barrier.

Headmaster Cresthill sat hunched over his desk, his forehead resting in an open palm. "Alright," he sighed, too exhausted to argue any further, "where and when would you like me to round up the students?"

"The guards that accompanied me have already begun to do so under the order of Her Grace," Elbar answered sheepishly. "They should all be gathered in the rotunda of Valethoran Hall."

Cresthill sighed audibly and rolled his eyes. "So your point in coming here was to do what, Tavon? Round me up and drag me along?"

"Essentially, yes..." Elbar replied. "Her Grace wishes you to be present on the mezzanine as she gives her address."

The Headmaster nodded slowly as he stood up from his desk. "Very well, I suppose. Let's not keep this whole thing waiting, then. I'm tired enough of it as it stands."

The rotunda of Valethorean Hall was typically abuzz with people. The centrepoint of the university, and the building from which the entire campus was built, it was rare that someone studying arcana in Lohvast went a week without at least passing their feet across the hall's marble floors. Had one been able to stack a week's worth of the daily hubub altogether, however, it would not amount to the scene that greeted Headmaster Cresthill and Archmage Elbar. Not accounting for the arcanists that had been called from the university already, Valethorean Hall was packed wall-to-wall with everybody who attended in any capacity.

"Your men certainly didn't waste any time, Tavon," the Headmaster remarked as the pair entered the rotunda. Despite the hint of dark irreverence in his tone, Cresthill could not help but admit to himself that the sight was equally as impressive as the expedience with which it had been conjured.

"You show such contempt for this kingdom, Daylen, and yet your life and livelihood are a direct result of living within the Lohvastine border," Elbar countered as they ascended the stairs to the mezzanine. "There are arcanists who could only dream to be able to make a life here. You are living in the intellectual hub of the Four Kingdoms!"

The pair reached the mezzanine. Royal guards and War Mages, all wearing the Lohvastine flag, stood along the railing of the semicircular platform, leaving a twenty foot wide gap in the middle, the leftmost point of which was to be occupied by Elbar and Cresthill. "Make no mistake," the Headmaster leaned in and whispered to his former colleague as the two stood looking out at the hundreds of faces below, "I am aware of the favourable path my life has taken. However, I am also aware that there have been strange goings-on, and whispers of grave plans that I can only hope are just that. As much as I wish my apprehensions to be unjustified, I have yet to see evidence that they are."

The crowd fell into a sudden hush, as did the Archmage and the Headmaster as Queen Merrian Arkalis strode toward the centre of the mezzanine. She was flanked by her personal bodyguards, two War Mages handpicked by the queen on her coronation fifteen years prior. In spite of her small stature and slender build, the queen walked with both grace and authority as she approached the railing, resting her hands gently upon the dark polished wood. She looked to either side of her, then down toward her captive audience. She smirked, basking for a moment in the silent attention, and began to speak.

"Ladies and gentlemen, I fear I must begin this address with a truly heartfelt apology." There were some confused murmurs in the crowd for a moment, until the queen raised her hand, prompting the crowd back into silence. "As many of you know," she continued, "I was born and raised an arcanist, and spent the better part of my adolescence here at this very institution. And yet, it has been six long years since I last was able to afford myself the opportunity to return. I apologize for two reasons. First, I ask that you forgive that I have not been as active an alum as this university deserves, and I beg you understand that my absence has not been of my accord, but has been an unfortunate sacrifice I have had to make in order to ensure that all of Lohvast continues to be the Crown of the World." Applause began to break out throughout the crowd, which the queen allowed to continue for a moment before raising her hand once more, causing the crowd to fall silent again.

"I fear, however, that this is only the easy, painless half of my apology," Arkalis' face took on a somber expression as she continued. "Though I have been very much looking forward to my return to these walls, I regret to say that my joy has been weighed down by the dark news that I bring with me.

It is with a heavy heart that I inform all of you here that Archmage Derrus Tyn of Hallowspire is dead." Gasps and murmurs bubbled upward from the rotunda floor, though this time the queen made no effort to silence the crowd before continuing. "What's more, I fear the Archmage's untimely end may have been not only intentional, but planned and executed from within the walls of Castle Rheth!" As the queen continued, the crowd lulled some, though several whispers could be heard throughout as she continued to deliver her news.

"This may shock many of you, I know," Arkalis raised her hand sympathetically as she spoke, "but it is no surprise to anyone that Hallowspire, and King Renton himself, have not held a high opinion of the arcane arts for decades now. In fact, I had received word not two months ago that, beyond the kingdom's barbaric laws against fae and lycanthropic beings, and it's ridiculous constraints on the use of arcana, King Renton passed a law banning all objects *potentially* of arcane or fae origin. I will admit, for a long while I had tried at relations with King Renton, thinking that perhaps through the joining of our hands and our kingdoms, I might educate him in all the ways that arcana has benefited our lives. I fear, however, that his Grace's actions of late have only confirmed my greatest fears. I fear that it is only a matter of time before the people of Hallowspire aim their bigotry outwards, and use steel to do so."

The crowd's volume raised at this, slightly above the level it had been before the Queen had entered the Hall. Again, she made no effort to quell the noise, choosing instead to raise her own voice above the din as she continued.

"As your queen, as an arcanist, and most importantly as a proud citizen of this kingdom, I refuse to sit idly by and allow our way of life be threatened by the violent ignorance of our neighbours. As such, I decree that we deal with this problem quickly, and at its source. We must make a stand against Hallowspire, and send King Renton Isevahr a powerful message: Lohvast will not fall under his heel!"

With this, the crowd in the rotunda of Valethorean Hall erupted in rounds of applause and thunderous cheering. Queen Arkalis allowed for the faintest curl at the corner of her lip, subtle enough so as not to belie her stern exterior. Finally, after several moments, she raised her hand once more to silence the audience.

"I am touched, truly, by your show of support in the face of such dire news. Such support will be not only necessary, but vital in the coming months. Some of you may have taken notice of the absence of certain members of the staff and faculty throughout these halls in the past weeks. I wish to inform you that these brave men and women have, indeed, committed their time, and though I dare not say it, potentially their lives to our noble cause. If the warmth and support you all have just shown me is an indication of what all within Lohvast are capable of, then I can happily report that our victory will not only be swift, but assured."

The final round of applause filled the room like a presence unto itself, so much so that even the Headmaster found himself applauding the speech. The noise continued as Queen Arkalis dipped a low curtsey, and turned to descend the stairs, her retinue in tow. Archmage Elbar and Headmaster Cresthill were the last to leave the rotunda, bowing ceremonially to the continued applause before following behind the royal train.

"Does her Grace plan on traveling throughout the kingdom to deliver this speech?" the Headmaster leaned in to Elbar as they descended the stairs.

The Archmage shook his head. "Local lords and ladies are doing most of the legwork, so to speak, but her Grace insisted on addressing the University herself, as in her words, 'the Arcanists are the key asset in all of this. If we do not have their unwavering support, then we, and the mission, are at a grave loss.'"

Cresthill pondered on this as he began to break from the train to return to his office, only to feel Archmage Elbar's hand on his shoulder. "One last thing," Elbar said. "Her Grace wishes for a personal audience with you."

Chapter 3

The arcane university in Lohvast was an expansive place. Even when Hallowspire and Ghest both boasted universities of their own, and both institutions were at their peaks of prominence, their sizes combined would have still paled in comparison to the the university in Lohvast. Some called the institution a small town, and yet the strange layout and masonry were more like that of a city talked about in stories of far-flung places where humans did not tread. It was a place that one could easily get turned around and lost in, even if one was careful. The university's headmaster, however, walked the winding paths the way animals traversed the most dense woods. The Headmaster had spent the last three-and-a-half decades maneuvering through the ever-expanding university, and knew every inch of it better than he knew the names of half the faculty, which is why anyone who saw him walking toward his meeting with Queen Merrian Arkalis would have been confused by the puzzled look on his face.

The look on Headmaster Cresthill's face was two-fold. On the one hand, the Headmaster was pensive toward the fact that the Queen had requested an audience with him in the first place. He had already given her and her cause substantial resources, and he was hesitant to commit any more, though he was aware that he had little choice in the matter. On the other hand, when Archmage Elbar had told Cresthill that the Queen's request that they meet in her personal accommodations, he had assumed that the Queen was staying in one of the more opulent residential buildings, possibly even the faculty residence, all of which were located near the heart of the campus. Instead, the Headmaster was instructed that the meeting would take place in a small cottage on the northeastern outskirts of the university. The cottage was something of a curiosity; decades prior, when the university had begun rapid outward expansion, it had bought the cottage and the surrounding land from an older shepherd, but due to numerous fiscal decisions in the years that followed, the land had yet to be touched. Attempts to sell the land were for naught, as nobody was interested in buying land from an institution that was sure to wish for it back at a later date. As a result, the cottage simply sat, unused, just off the university campus, while technically being a part of it.

Headmaster Cresthill approached the cabin, knocking on the faded wood of the front door. He was greeted by a member of the Queen's personal guards, one of the rare cases in which Arkalis used manpower in favour of arcana. The large man examined the Headmaster a moment, saying nothing before turning inward. "Your Grace," he called out in the deep, professional voice of a man with years of military training, "Headmaster Daylen Cresthill has arrived!"

"Lead him in, Captain," Queen Arkalis called back in contrast, her voice noticeably more casual and almost melodic in comparison to her guard's stoic tone. The guard did as he was told, remaining silent as he led Cresthill down the main hallway to a moderate-sized room at the back of the cottage where Queen Arkalis stood, her back to the doorway, warming herself in front of a small fireplace hearth. "As you were, Captain, thank you," she said without turning. The guard bowed, still silent, and turned about-face, exiting the room.

"Your Grace wished to speak with me?" the Headmaster bowed low, still standing in the threshold of the room.

The Queen turned around, smiling broadly as her long plum-coloured gown fanned out behind her. "Daylen Cresthill, how the years have been kind to you." She walked toward the centre of the room, beckoning the Headmaster forward. "From prominent professor to Headmaster in, by the gods, how long have I been away?"

"Six years since you completed your studies, your Grace," the Headmaster offered as he walked further into the room.

"Please, Daylen," the Queen smiled warmly as she placed a hand on the Headmaster's shoulder. "Whenever I studied under you during my time at the university, you refused to refer to me by any of my titles, and I feel that I wound up the better for it. Within the confines of the university, I see you as an equal, if not still as a superior. Do not feel obligated to treat me any differently than you had six years ago."

"As you wish... Merrian." Cresthill tried to read the Queen's face at this, but she simply remained smiling. "You wished to see me?"

"Yes," she responded "I wished to thank you personally for everything you have done recently."

"Oh?"

"Archmage Elbar has spoken at length about the grace you have shown in accommodating the requests I have given of you and the university of late. These last months have been some of the most difficult I have endured, between the news of Derrus, and now going to war with Hallowspire! I cannot tell you how many sleepless nights I have had, worrying if I made the right choice, or worse, if Lohvast feels I made the wrong one..." she trailed off, her smile accented by the lonely, worrisome eyes only seen by those in positions of great authority and responsibility. It was a look the Headmaster was not expecting from a woman who, as long as he had known her, was more often than not a portrait of confidence.

"Come now, Merrian," the soothing tone of the Headmaster's words resulted in a more comfortable eschew of formality. "I was standing not twenty feet from you as you delivered your address, I saw the crowd's reaction. You've nothing to fear."

"Don't I, Daylen?" Her deep blue eyes maintained their look of despair as they met his. "I attended the university. By the gods, I studied under its current Headmaster. I have a presence here, but I cannot have that kind of presence throughout Lohvast. What am I to the average farmer or artisan, but some shadowy figurehead who takes their taxes and may now be endangering their well-being?"

"Merrian, listen to yourself." Cresthill's gaze did not break from the Queen's. "Now it is no secret amid the university that I am not exactly the model of civic pride, but I'd be damned if I did not admit that, by and large, the people of Lohvast have a notably high quality of life, thanks in no small part to a Queen who has historically made a point of putting the needs of her people first. Anybody who does not trust your judgment in this will not only be seen a fool, but will be part of a small minority thereof."

The Queen sighed audibly, looking down, and then back up to the Headmaster, as though some of the weight had been lifted from her mind. "Thank you, Daylen. Your support in this means worlds to me." She placed her hand on his as if to accentuate her statement. "This war will be trying in many ways, and I will need strong, trustworthy allies by my side, some of whom," she paused mid-sentence, and without breaking her gaze, lifted the Headmaster's hand to her lips and kissed it. "I wish to keep notably closer than others."

The Headmaster looked at the Queen, his mind now a vortex of confusion. "Merrian, I... what..." he stammered, taken so off-guard by this that he was unable to collect his thoughts into something coherent.

"You should not be so shocked," the Queen smiled sweetly. "I am nearly halfway to thirty and still unmarried, and what better a show of solidarity for the people of Lohvast than for their Queen to take the head of our most prominent institution as a husband?"

"I am twice your age," Cresthill attempted to protest.

"And yet you've the look of someone ten years your junior," the Queen replied, "and I've no doubt the virility to match. Besides," she added, her smile now slightly less innocent, "I am fully aware of the passing glances I received all too often when I was a student."

"By the gods, I had a wife!"

"Something that is no longer here nor there, may she be among the gods." The Queen took a step closer, looking up only inches away from the Headmaster's face. "Daylen, I do not expect an answer this instant, only that you ponder on it. I will be remaining at the university for two more days, please come back to see me before I am off." She leaned in and whispered, "I will be waiting."

The Queen backed away, and the Headmaster, trying his utmost not to blush, bowed low. "In two days then... Merrian." He excused himself and exited, leaving the Queen to return to her fire.

"You've certainly given him some food for thought," a voice spoke out from the shadows. "Though, aren't you a bit worried you may have offered the old man a feast he won't have the stomach to handle?"

"Generally speaking," the Queen responded, "men's eyes tend to be larger than their appetites. And besides, I meant everything I said. I simply omitted how the union would serve Lohvast and the Mission in equal measure. Further," she added, "I asked the Headmaster to drop the formalities, but I do not recall imparting that privilege onto you."

"Apologies, your Grace," Lannister Ravenclaw bowed apologetically as he emerged from the shadows. "What is the plan?"

"Follow the Headmaster," the Queen responded, her eyes fixated on the fire. "Keep an eye on his actions until he returns to me with his answer. If he does anything to jeopardize the Mission, kill him."

"And if he returns with an answer that's not to your Grace's liking, should I kill him then?"

"No," she responded coolly. "In such an eventuality, I will deal with the matter personally."

Chapter 4

Following the attempted goblin ransacking, Adrik had made the decision to keep his cart as far away from the more densely wooded areas along the main trade road as possible. The dwarf's detour added substantial time to their travels, and as a result, the group found themselves roughly a full day's travel from East Fellowdale by nightfall. Opting not to push on through the night, the companions stopped in their destination's sister city, West Fellowdale. "This is the older of the two cities," O'doc explained as the group made their way into the city centre, "but it never managed to reach the size and scope of its eastern twin."

"I do remember hearing something to that effect in my travels," Adrik responded. "The Baron Franz Helpatz the Fourth had twin heirs, Mats and Greta. When the pair came of age, they were to divide ownership of the city, then still no larger than a village, evenly, but did not as the result of a long-standing dispute of some kind or the other. As a result, Greta set out with a small group and founded her own village on the shores of the Ghestal Sea. Of course, as trade came to rely consistently more heavily on the use of seafaring vessels, East soon dwarfed West, but the origin of its founding is why, despite their noticeable discrepancies in size, they are know as the Twin Cities of Ghest."

O'doc stared blankly at the dwarf with his mouth somewhat agape. "I grew up north of East Fellowdale, and I don't think I could have given that much information... where, by the gods, did you learn all that?"

"Remember, Master O'doc, that despite my youthful exuberance, I am many tens of years your senior. My time on the road has done nothing if not widened me with each passing day." Adrik pulled the reigns of his wagon, bringing his mules to a stop outside a building with lit windows, the sound of bustle, a sign depicting a foaming mug sitting atop a fireplace hearth. "This seems a fine enough establishment in which to rest our weary bones."

After tying off the wagon, the group walked through the large wooden door into the tavern. Adrik led the group through the crowded taproom, striding easily through a myriad of people of varying races, his eyes transfixed on the bar, whereby the group could find themselves a bite to eat and a room for the night. O'doc stayed close, keeping his head low and the hood of his cloak pulled up for fear of a River Rat sighting, while Erasmus ventured off to find one of the few unoccupied tables. Enna did everything within her power to try and look as casual as her companions, but was having a difficult time doing so. Everything about the moment was something the young elf had never experienced before. Scores of conversations being spoken in numerous languages and accents, with humans and halflings mingling easily with dwarves, elves, and even a few half-orcs and gnomes. Enna was so overwhelmed that she did not realize the large half-orc standing in front of her, in spite of unknowingly gazing wide-eyed in his direction.

"Keep moving, faeling," the half-orc bellowed, snapping Enna from her trance. "You ain't my type. I like my girls with some meat on 'em. Last time I bedded an elf I split her right down the middle." Enna quickly brought her eyes forward, her face beginning to flush with embarrassment, and opted to join Erasmus in a search for a table. The elf wove through the crowd with more tact than she had used a moment earlier, and soon spotted the bard sitting relaxed at a round table off to one side of the taproom, wistfully taking in the scenery.

"You seem right at home," Enna said as she took a seat next to him.

"Taverns have always been where I made my living," Erasmus replied, his tone somewhat reminiscent. "As soon as I could play well enough, I took stages. If the stages were occupied, I tried my luck at cards or dice."

"Did you charm the coins out of the gamblers' pockets, as well?" Enna playfully chided. The question was met with a dirty look.

"I relied on my own luck and natural skill, I will have you know," the half-elf responded defensively.

"I have to agree with him," O'doc interjected as he and Adrik arrived at the table, drinks in either hand. "He just isn't mentioning that his luck is piss-poor, and he's naturally skilled at being a terrible cheater." The pair sat down, doling out the drinks accordingly. "I admit my crack about the luck might be debatable, though. Were it not for Erasmus being a terrible cheat, we may never have crossed paths."

"This sounds as though it has the makings of quite the amusing anecdote," Adrik mused, taking a long drink and slapping Erasmus on the back as he glowered at his partner. "Please, master O'doc, continue."

O'doc, now more comfortable after having not seen any familiar faces, pulled back the hood of his cloak. "The story begins in a tavern not dissimilar to this one. I had recently cut my ties with Lannister Ravenclaw, and was enjoying the freedom and independence that goes along with the lifestyle I'd chosen, and was looking to increase my profits for the day with a few games of Captain's Gambit. I was four hands into a six-man game when I notice someone enter the tavern, soaked to the bone from the storm outside. He doesn't look particularly well-off, so I don't pay him much mind after that."

"Now, two more hands pass by, and who should join the table, but a scruffy-looking half-elf, trying his all not to look like a child eying a jam tart as he looks at the game."

"I had been at sea for the last two weeks..." Erasmus protested.

"And you've got a bit too heavy a soft spot for cards and dice," O'doc added quickly.

"You're enjoying this, aren't you?" the half-elf countered, trying to keep his tone nonchalant. While the question was directed at O'doc, the whole table nodded their assent.

"Moving ahead roughly half an hour, poor Erasmus has lost roughly three out of every four hands he plays. What's more, there's been another addition to the table. An absolute beauty of an elven woman." O'doc made a curvaceous motion with his hands to demonstrate his point, causing Enna to roll her eyes.

"Now, she and Erasmus can barely keep their eyes off one another, but not how you might think. Anyone at the table would have been able to tell you the two knew each other, and the tension was thicker than fog in mid spring. Both tried to play it off, making the kind of idle table talk one does, until this one," O'doc thumbed at Erasmus, "tries slipping an extra trump into his hand. Only trouble is that this dwarf longshoreman sitting next to me already had both in his hand, and made a point of calling out Erasmus' sleight with a knife. So the table gets upturned, and a full-on brawl breaks out."

"And everyone in the tavern just let it happen?" Enna stared in disbelief.

"Milady, such an occurrence is so commonplace in certain locales, one would think it quite the anomaly if there were fewer than three over a fortnight," Adrik chuckled. "So, Master O'doc, how did this brawl result in the serendipitous partnership of you two rapscallions?"

"Now this is the interesting bit," O'doc continued, pausing only to take a drink. "So this brawl's broken out, fists, feet, and bottles flying all about, and amid it all, there's Erasmus having a chat with that elf, seemingly oblivious to what's going on around him, including the dwarf, who was now making his way though the crowd, aiming to put that knife in Erasmus' back. Now, I'm not the first person to be talking about honour, but the idea of a man getting knifed in the kidney over a card game just doesn't sit well with me, especially if it's from behind. So, I did what any sane individual would do when faced with that situation, and tackled an angry dwarf with a knife to save a cheating stranger from getting gutted."

"Naturally," Adrik conceded, still chuckling.

"So, anyway, after I tackled the dwarf, I did what I could to drag Erasmus out of that tavern, and the rest is history." O'doc raised his mug to toast his partner, who smirked at the halfling, and eventually obliged.

"A fine tale, indeed," Adrik bellowed, then raising his own mug. "To the bonds of friendship, forged in situations most extraordinary!" The companions all toasted, taking long drinks thereafter.

"One question, though," Enna said, placing her own drink down on the table. "Who was the elven woman you were talking to?"

"You know, that's an excellent question," O'doc mused. "In all our years working together, I never asked you that. I just assumed from body language that she was an old fling or something like that."

Erasmus looked down into his drink, his expression now one of wistful nostalgia. "Something like that," he nodded, before looking back up. "I seem to be out of a drink," he said as he stood up. "The next round is on me."

Chapter 5

The companions left West Fellowdale early the next morning, and when the wagon approached its sister city a few hours later, all were thankful for the relative quiet in the interim. East Fellowdale was markedly larger, noticeably comparable to Rheth, which caused Enna to be surprised when O'doc informed her that the port city was not Ghest's capital.

"As Adrik mentioned the other night, West Fellowdale is a younger city than many in Ghest," the halfling explained. "When the nation was united under the Van Hyden banner, its main trade partners were the dwarven thanes to the south, and as such King Tillman Van Hyden founded Tillburg near the southeastern Otharines, claiming it the capital."

Enna nodded, taking in the information, all the while trying not to be overwhelmed by the sights. She was unable to contain an audible gasp, however, as the wagon wound across a number of streets before pulling onto a road that traveled dockside. The elf was awestruck as the wagon rolled down the road alongside rows of tallships. The ships, however, did not quite cause Enna as much pause as the vast blue expanses that stretched out behind them.

"She's quite the view, isn't she?" O'doc smiled, catching himself gazing seaward as well. "Get used to waking up to it for a while, this is where we'll be staying." The halfling motioned Adrik to pull the cart to a stop out front of a tall stonework tavern. A wooden sign hung above the tavern door depicting a man in nautical garb and a scaly, green-skinned woman.

"The Sailor and Seahag, eh?" Erasmus chuckled.

"It's not that bad," O'doc protested. "Besides, it wasn't my choice. My contact insisted on meeting here."

"Really?" the half-elf raised his eyebrows, still smiling. "I'm starting to worry about who this contact of yours is."

"Oh, stop it," O'doc scowled as he hopped off the cart and began to tie up the mules. "You'll make these two think we'll need to lock and bar our doors overnight."

"Speak for yourself," Erasmus countered, helping to unload the cart. "If this place and its patrons are anything like the last time I was here, I'd be better off leaving my door wide open and letting the women come and go as they please."

"O'doc, I thought you said Erasmus lost money on games, not women," Enna said, forcing Adrik to stifle a hearty laugh as the group rounded up what they needed before entering the tavern.

The taproom of the Sailor and Seahag smelled of stale porter and unwashed sailors, and anyone unfortunate enough to misstep into an errant sticky spot or burly mariner would be able to pinpoint the source of the smell. In spite of the grizzly appearance, however, there was an air of joviality in the taproom, most evident when the companions walked up to the bar to secure lodging. The group was met by a young dwarf with a short, well-groomed beard, who introduced himself as Fenril Finehead.

"You lot don't look like seafaring sorts," the dwarf commented as he took out a large leather-bound ledger from behind the bar. "What brings you to the Seahag?"

"Meeting a friend," O'doc answered, drawing his coin purse out from the folds of his cloak.

Fenril nodded, taking everyone's names as he took their coins, stopping after writing Enna's name down, and eying the coins surreptitiously. "Not to pry..." Fenril said, "but you lot never mentioned where you were from..."

"Ah, the coins!" Erasmus softly hit his forehead as though he had just been reminded of something. "Nothing nefarious, I can assure you. I recently spent a month performing in Pheasantkeep just along the western boarder." The half-elf raised his mandolin case up. "If you like, I could maybe offer some entertainment to your patrons while we're in town?"

The dwarf paused a moment to consider the offer, before smiling broadly and sliding a few coins back over the bar. "There are four rooms at the end of the hall on the third floor, they're all yours. This place gets busy right near sunset, I hope you're as good as you say."

"That seemed a bit odd," Enna commented as the group ascended the stairs toward their rooms. "Was it my imagination, or did that barkeep seem suspicious after I told him my name?"

"I can't say I blame him," O'doc responded. "Strange enough a group as motley as ours wanders in here paying with Hallowspire coins, but when the elf of the group gives a human family name..."

Enna nodded thoughtfully at this. She was still getting used to being recognized as an elf. Her friends had explained to her early into their trip that humans and elves were physically similar enough that to the people of Hallowspire, who rarely if ever saw fae-folk, so Enna was easily passable as a human. Elsewhere in the Kingdoms, however, where the majority of races freely co-mingled, it was more easily assumed that someone of Enna's build was of fae descent.

"I wouldn't worry about it," Erasmus interjected. "He gave us our rooms, didn't he?"

"And at a discounted price, nonetheless," Adrik added, clapping the half-elf on the back.

"Maybe you're right," O'doc conceded. "That barkeep wasn't here the last time I was in town. Maybe he's just new, being extra cautious."

The companions reached their rooms, at the far end of the third-floor hall, two on either side. "Well, I cannot speak for you, friends," Adrik stated, stretching his stout arms into the air, "but I feel in need of some freshening up before our fateful rendezvous."

"When is your contact supposed to meet us?" Enna asked O'doc, trying not to belie her nerves.

"After dark," O'doc answered. "We're in no rush, so I vote in the meantime we head downstairs, try to make merry, and listen to some fine mandolin."

The companions ate a hearty meal of sausage and potatoes, and listened as Erasmus entertained the bustling tavern with all manner of song, ranging from local folk tunes and popular sea shanties, to longer pieces that recounted tales older than the Kingdoms, of great wars fought against giants and dragons. Enna listened to every word the bard sang, imagining the sights and sounds as though she were there. When she was a young girl, Enna's father would tell her tales of the places he'd been, of dwarves and elves, goblins and orcs. The lyrics coming from Erasmus were of something different altogether. Randis had never seen a giant or a dragon, and as far as Enna knew, very few people ever had.

She imagined herself, one day, being able to mimic the fantastic arcane feats that were unfolding in her mind's eye. Enna had been studying Varis' old spellbooks for weeks, and was still able to do little more than light a candle or float a small rock in midair for less than a minute. She thought back to Rheth, when she conjured a great gale in the streets, and wished she could understand what she had done different then.

The elf was pulled from her thoughts by a thunderous round of applause as Erasmus finished his performance. The half-elf took several deep bows before walking from the makeshift stage near the far side of the bar and joining his friends at their table.

"A fine performance, my good man!" Adrik clapped Erasmus on the shoulder as he sat.

"Ah, he was a bit off-key during the second half," O'doc teased. "What do you think, Enna? How did our boy fare?"

Enna smiled and opened her mouth to answer, trying to think of how to explain that she had spent the better part of the performance daydreaming, when O'doc's eyes moved directly behind her. Enna turned to see a small figure in a cloak and hood standing just behind her.

"Is there somewhere we can speak quietly?" the hooded halfling woman asked. Her voice was not youthful, but not markedly aged, either. By Enna's estimation, this woman was likely not much older than her own parents. There was also a refinement in the tone that was noticeably incongruous with the majority of the surrounding clientele.

"Of course," O'doc answered. "We've each a room two floors up. We can use mine." The halfling stood up and lead the way, his contact behind him, and Erasmus, Adrik, and Enna taking up the rear. The five of them inside O'doc's room made the area snug, but not uncomfortable. When all were inside and O'doc locked his door, the halfling woman removed her hood to reveal a kind, deceptively youthful face, crowned with silver braided hair.

"You look well, O'doc," she said, smiling warmly and opening her arms to him.

"Hello, aunt Caliope," he responded, stepping into her embrace. "How have you been keeping?"

"Aunt?" Erasmus raised a quizzical eyebrow. "O'doc, we've been through this town how many times since we became partners, and never once did you mention that you have family living here."

"And with good cause," O'doc replied. "This town has always been lousy with Rats, and the last thing I needed was for anyone to know anything about my family."

"I cannot say that I am thrilled about lurking in the shadows to see my nephew," Caliope added, a hint of admonishment in her voice. "I have told you on multiple occasions that the temple of Bremmer is a safe place, and offers me protection, as it would do for you."

O'doc shook his head resolutely. "Were that it was enough. The River Rats are ruthless, aunt, and not even the sanctity of holy ground would hold them back. Never mind what they would do if they connected you to mom and dad, and the others."

Caliope's lips pursed into a frown of disapproval and grim understanding in equal measure. She sighed heavily before turning to Enna, a warm smile reappearing. "Am I safe to assume that you are the lovely young lady that O'doc has contacted me about?"

"I imagine so," Enna replied, dipping as much of a curtsey as she could in the small space. "Enna Summerlark, milady."

"A curiously human name for an elf, my dear," Caliope noted, returning the curtsey.

"Elven born," Enna brushed the hair away from one ear and removed the pointed golden cuff atop it, revealing a shorter, rounded-off scar, "but human raised."

Caliope's eyes widened at the sight. "So that's how..." she whispered before approaching Enna and taking her hand. "Oh you poor dear..." Enna smiled and thanked the halfling for her compassion, explaining to her the story behind the scars, and assuring her that they were not the result of malevolence. "So you have no knowledge of your birth parents, or of your native kin?" she asked.

Enna shook her head. "Only a physical description of my birth mother, and little more than half-whispered fairy stories about elves as a people. I was hoping to gain some information from you."

Caliope looked sidelong at O'doc. "Is that what my nephew told you?"

Enna's confused gaze joined Caliope's. "Well, I mean... not exactly. He just... he said he had a friend here that knew about fae-folk, and then he referred to you as his contact... I just sort of assumed..."

Caliope stared at O'doc and shook her head as half-smile appeared on her face. "I would advise you to avoid assumptions where my nephew is concerned, my dear." She returned her eyes to Enna. "I love him to death, but you must practically throttle straight answers out of him." O'doc smirked sheepishly at this. "While I would love to help you, Enna, the truth is I am more of a go-between. I have something of a knack for knowing everything that goes on within these city walls, so whenever O'doc needs information for the right reasons..." the halfling paused to look again at O'doc, her eyes and tone slightly more stern than before, "he gets in touch with me, and I get in touch with whoever I know that might be helpful."

"And whom might that be on this particular occasion?" Erasmus asked, still coming to terms with the fact that he seemed to know less about his partner than he thought.

"A very close, very dear friend," Caliope responded. "Well-versed both in arcana and in the fae."

"Professor Falken Coldstone," O'doc added, inciting a short laugh from Erasmus.

"Are you serious?" the half-elf chuckled. "You claim to know everyone in this city, a city that used to boast a reputable arcane university, and you mean to send us to the one faculty member to ever be kicked out?"

"Under false pretenses!" Caliope defended bitterly. "Headmaster Riverwall was a fool presiding over a failing institution. It only made sense that when problems arose from within, he would find the one odd duck in the faculty and make a scapegoat of him." She shook her head sympathetically before looking back to Erasmus. "And if my memory serves, I was asked to look for help for a young lady looking for answers, not her sharp-tongued, dim-witted cohort who apparently has all the answers he needs."

Erasmus moved to argue, but was stopped by Adrik, who held his hand out to keep the half-elf at bay. "You will have to excuse Master Stonehand, milady. He speaks only out of concern, though he doubtless lacks milady's nuanced understanding of East Fellowdale's population."

"My apologies, as well," Caliope nodded. "I, too, have a tendency of showing such concern for my friends, their reputations included." She turned back to Enna. "I can take you to the professor's manor tonight, if that suits you, my dear."

Enna nodded and smiled. "That would be wonderful, thank you Caliope."

The halfling smiled back. "You're quite welcome." The group moved to exit the room, Caliope stopping before opening the door. "Now, I should offer you some fair warning. Professor Coldstone is as warm and welcoming as he is knowledgeable, but he is not without his eccentricities. I suggest you try your best not to dwell on them."

Chapter 6

In the days that followed the proposal Queen Merrian had presented him, Daylen Cresthill spent most of his time deep in thought, and Lannister Ravenclaw had, unbeknownst to the Headmaster, spent most of his time patiently observing. After the two days had passed, Cresthill returned to the old cottage on the outskirts of the arcane university, was greeted, as before, by a guard who guided him into the same room where Cresthill and the Queen spoke prior. This time, Queen Merrian sat in a tall, plush wingback chair, sipping from a crystal cup filled with wine.

"Ah, Daylen!" she smiled, setting the cup down on a small table next to her. "I have quite been looking forward to your visit today."

"As have I, Merrian." the Headmaster smiled back in an attempt to belie his nervousness. "I have been doing quite a great deal of thinking regarding our last meeting."

"Oh?" The Queen raised one eyebrow playfully.

"You raised several good points when last we spoke. A marriage would doubtless boost national morale, and given the importance Lohvast places on arcana, a union between you and I ostensibly makes good sense. Further, you have made it clear that there is something of a mutual attraction between us."

"I am so glad you agree, Daylen," the Queen cooed.

"Please, allow me to finish." The Headmaster raised his hand. "Having taken all this into consideration, I cannot accept your hand."

"Really?" both the Queen's eyebrows raised with surprise, though her tone remained even and composed. "Why is that, Daylen?"

The Headmaster swallowed nervously. "Merrian, you are a queen on the brink of taking your people to war. You are young, unmarried, and ambitious. Your hand is coveted by noble men from one side of Lohvast to the other. I am an ignoble widower who, while I hold a position of stature among arcanists, possesses no formal title whatsoever. To take my hand in marriage would be a tremendous sleight to many, many noble families, some of whom may be so spurned as to withhold their support in the oncoming war. I implore you, Merrian, wait until this business with Hallowspire is done, and I will be here, if you would have me."

The Queen stood up and began to glide toward the headmaster, the train of her sleek silvery gown trailing behind her. She smiled warmly at Cresthill as she approached him, placing a hand on his shoulder. "Of course, you are right, Daylen. I only wish that this did not complicate matters so."

"How do you mean?"

The Queen looked the headmaster deep in his dark eyes, and he saw her's flash a deep crimson hue. She spoke in a whisper, but the voice was not her own. It was as though, from her body, the voices of many spoke.

"*Jilg jacida gewjlei ekess sia geou.*"

Daylen Cresthill stood wide-eyed for a moment. Though he could not understand the words, he knew the tongue to be dark and infernal. His mind wanted to race, to sort through his years of accumulated knowledge and find the exact source and reasoning behind the words, but in a fraction of a second the Headmaster's thoughts were brought to a halt. Cresthill fell to one knee as Queen Merrian's hand clutched his shoulder, and he cried out in agony as he felt a searing pain from beneath his skin rise to the surface.

When the Queen removed her hand, the cried of pain stopped, and Cresthill stood, his eyes now pools of black as they met her own.

"When you return to your quarters, you will remember nothing of what happened since my formal address at Valethorean Hall. You will carry on your duties as headmaster as normal. However, when my voice enters your mind, you shall be as you are now: at my beck and call."

The Headmaster nodded, but before the Queen could bid him away, Lannister Ravenclaw slunk into the room.

"Excellent," Queen Merrian smiled. "Guildmaster, escort Headmaster Cresthill to his room."

The halfling bowed. "A word with your Grace first, if it pleases you. One of my men in East

Fellowdale has apparently spotted my sell-swords, as well as the elf from Hallowspire."

"Guildmaster, we are preparing to march on Hallowspire's westernmost borders. Surely you understand that there are much greater matters at hand."

"Your Grace, if I don't act now, the opportunity may be lost. O'doc Overhill is a tricky bastard, and he'll know how to keep that elf safe. Let me act on this, I could succeed where Derrus Tyn failed."

"Derrus Tyn was a fool on a fool's errand!" Queen Merrian snapped. "Now he is little more than ash stuck to the floor of some dank cell below Rheth. Do not assume that you are immune to a similar fate."

"I swore an oath to serve the Mission, the same as you," Ravenclaw hissed. "I was promised revenge against those who wronged me, and here I have a chance to exact it, and stay true to that oath. You would deny me that for no other reason than to have me babysit your personal man-slave? Which one of us is really serving the Mission, your Grace?"

Queen Merrian's eyes flashed a bright, furious red, boring into the halfling. Ravenclaw winced only slightly as he felt a familiar heat in his left shoulder. "You insolent little cretin..." the Queen spoke through clenched teeth. Seeing that the halfling was giving no quarter, The Queen broke her gaze, causing the pain in Ravenclaw's shoulder to dissipate. The Queen placed her thumb and forefinger on the bridge of her nose in exasperation. "See the Headmaster to his quarters," she said with a hint of defeat in her voice, "then deal with your little problem in Ghest. You are free to use whatever resources your filthy guild has at its disposal, but you are to remain in Lohvast."

"As you wish, your Grace." Ravenclaw bowed low, his mouth caught in a smug sneer. He stood up and made a flourishing gesture toward the door. "After you, Headmaster."

Headmaster Cresthill methodically walked toward the exit of the room, his eyes ever-forward. As Ravenclaw began to walk behind him, he stopped at the voice of the Queen.

"You are as clever as you are resourceful, Guildmaster," she spoke coldly. "Make no mistake, though, there is a very real hierarchy among us, and your insolence will only be outweighed by your assets for so long."

"What you see as insolence, I see as ambition," the halfling retorted, not looking back. "A quality that, along with my other assets, has always managed to get me what I want in this world." He pulled the hood of his cloak over his head and began to stride out. "Goodnight, your Grace."

Chapter 7

The sun had dipped behind the buildings of East Fellowdale as the companions followed Caliope through the winding streets. It was not long before the group reached a fairly large manor at the corner of two major intersecting roads. The older halfling led the way past the gate and up to the large wooden front door.

"He is expecting us," Caliope smiled as she knocked twice at the door. A moment later there was the noise on the other end of a number of locks and latches being unfastened, before the door swung inward to reveal Professor Falken Coldstone.

"Ah, wonderful, you are all here!" The professor said, a hint of surprise in his voice as he attempted to smooth his hair with one hand, motioning the group to enter with the other. "Please, do come in!"

The professor cut a slightly different figure from what Enna had expected. The young elf expected someone much older, and judging by Erasmus' apprehension regarding the meeting, some old, frail-looking man with a long white beard and wild eyes. However, Coldstone appeared no older than perhaps a year or two past thirty, with a kind face devoid of facial hair save for small sideburns, and eyes that seemed at once present and distant.

"Please, everyone, I do beg your pardon for the state of my estate," the professor said as the group entered, allowing himself an amused snort at his unintentional play on words, "but I so rarely receive visitors, much less so many at a time." He led the group in single-file, precariously avoiding scattered books and parchments, to a fairly large kitchen in the manor's rear. There were several chairs tucked into a large wooden table at the kitchen's far end, most sporting a layer of dust along the backrests. The group all took seats around the table, which was cluttered much in the same fashion as the floors and walls, while the professor hung an iron kettle over an already burning fire in the hearth.

"Well then," he said, spinning around and clapping his hands together, "I do suppose introductions are in order. I, as you have all doubtless guessed, am Professor Falken Coldstone." The professor bowed low, causing his mustard-yellow robes to billow outward.

"Erasmus Stonehand," The bard smiled politely as he stretched his hand out to shake Coldstone's. He tried his best not to appear as though he was sizing the professor up, but a subtle elbow from O'doc let him know that his intentions were obvious enough, though perhaps not enough for Coldstone himself to notice.

Adrik bowed in his seat, removing his ratty tricorn hat with a sweeping motion. "Adrik Thornmallet at your service, Professor."

"Min bold sa ure bold, min ealu sa ure ealu." Coldstone said, returning the bow.

"Ure freod sa cyrten fand." Adrik responded almost ceremoniously before raising his head, his violet eyes now wide as they looked at Coldstone. "You know Dwarfish?"

"Enough to get by," the professor shrugged. "I'm afraid the proper accentuation still eludes me."

"Still, the best I have heard in some time." Adrik clapped the professor on the shoulder, nearly knocking him over. "Well met indeed, friend."

Coldstone smiled once more at the dwarf before turning to face Enna, his eyes full of curious wonder. "And you are she?" he asked, "The elf from Hallowspire?"

"I suppose my reputation precedes me," Enna smiled, bowing her head to the professor. "My name is Enna Summerlark."

"Ahh, a human name... how intriguing," the professor beamed, sitting next to Enna. "Please, my dear, you must elaborate! I am sure that your story is positively fascinating!"

"Not nearly as much as you might be expecting," Enna admitted, proceeding then to explain to the professor the mysterious circumstances of her birth, and explaining that she would have most likely gone on much longer not knowing of her true heritage, had it not been for her stumbling into her inherent gift for arcana.

"An arcanist, too?" Coldstone noted.

"I'd hardly say that," Enna replied. "I only just started studying it, really, and I know that being an elf gives me a bit of an advantage."

"Why do you say that, my dear?"

"Well, because..." Enna was about to continue, but quickly remembered what Varis had told she and Erasmus back in Rheth, how the relationship between arcana and the fae realm was a closely-guarded secret among the fae-folk. While Enna still maintained a much kinder view of the other races than Varis had when he was alive, she was cautious nonetheless. "I had been told that it was common knowledge that fae-folk happened to be inherently gifted with arcana."

"Ah," the professor nodded. "Quite right, quite right. You know, I had always had a theory about that."

"Really?" Erasmus couldn't help but interject. "Go on."

"Well, you see, I have always believed that..." The professor's explanation was cut short by the whistling sound of the kettle. "Oh blast," he said absentmindedly. "I forgot about the kettle." The professor then proceeded to pull a small, simple-looking wand from the folds of his cloak, point it at the whistling kettle and whisper the words, "*kalina vee' quesse willi ed' sina cam*". The kettle then lifted from the hearth and floated, guided by Coldstone's hand, onto a thick slab of stone set atop a wooden counter nearby. "Would anyone care for some hot cider?" he asked, looking about the room at his guests.

"That was amazing!" Enna gasped.

"Just a minor cantrip, really," the professor responded as he walked toward the kettle.

"Yes, don't go giving Falken here a swelled head," Caliope jested. "Some cider would be lovely, professor." Coldstone smiled and nodded, gathering a number of clay mugs from a nearby shelf.

"Well it's certainly worlds better than I can do," Enna responded, taking the warm mug offered to her by the professor. "I've been studying arcana for maybe a month now, and I have yet to float anything larger than a small stone.."

"My dear," Coldstone began as he handed mugs to the rest of his guests. "Arcana is something that is honed over years of practice. One does not simply learn to control the great arcane forces in..." He stopped a moment, and contemplated what Enna had said as he handed the last two mugs to the halflings at the far end of the table. "Did you say that you have only been studying arcana for a month?"

"Roughly, yes."

"That is extraordinary!" Coldstone shook his head. "The fae-folk truly are attuned to the arcane forces." He sat down next to Enna. "Please, show me something that you are capable of."

Enna nodded and stood up, facing the table. She took her small club from her belt and held it at her side in her right hand. Since leaving for Ghest, Enna had affixed to the club the small piece of green quartz from the necklace Adrik had given her as a child. Enna held her left arm outward, her palm open and facing up. Closing her eyes and concentrating, Enna felt energy begin to pulse from her club, which had begun to emit a faint green glow. She spoke the words *"Koron en' naur"*, and in an instant, felt a surge of energy shoot through her body, traveling from the club to her outstretched palm, and surfacing in the form of a small orb of yellow-orange flame that floated less than an inch from the surface of her palm.

The orb was there for only a moment before it dissipated, and Enna's arms and posture went slack. The elf breathed heavily as sweat glistened on her forehead. Everyone seated at the table had a shared look of disbelief on their faces.

"Enna," O'doc began, breaking a long moment of stunned silence. "When did you learn to do that?"

"I started really delving into Varis' books after the incident with the goblins," Enna replied breathlessly as she returned to her seat, visibly exhausted. "It's not even that powerful," she dismissed. "You all just saw what happened. It was there and then gone, and now I feel like I just tilled an acre of field by myself."

"Nonsense," Coldstone replied. "You have been studying arcana only a month, and already you are beginning to conjure fireballs. With the proper instruction you could become a truly gifted arcanist, Enna." The professor stood and looked at the group.

"For tonight, let us finish our drinks and get to know one another a little better. Much as I would love to dive right into the thick of things tonight, Enna's little display seems to have left her rather weary. Tomorrow evening, however, return for supper, and we shall spend the night trying our best to answer one another's questions. I trust we will all have much to learn from each other."

After roughly an hour of cider and small-talk, the group took their leave, bidding the professor good night, and later doing the same to Caliope as she returned to the temple of Bremmer. Finally, after returning to a still bustling Sailor and Seahag, Adrik, Enna, Erasmus, and O'doc bid one another good night as they returned to their respective rooms.

Adrik Thornmallet was in high spirits as he unlocked the door to his cozy room, but as he removed his ratty tricorn hat and placed it on a peg on the door, he felt a slight, chilly breeze cross his back. The dwarf did not remember leaving his room's window open, and as such he carefully reached for the small mace hanging from his belt, proceeding to spin on his heels and draw the weapon menacingly.

Adrik scanned the room easily due to the room's size and his natural acclimation to dim light. The window was indeed ajar, yet the dwarf was alone. Other than the open window, nothing was amiss, save for a piece of neatly folded parchment sitting underneath a small stone on the bedside table. Walking up closer to investigate, Adrik shut the window and drew the drape. Removing the stone, he picked up the piece of parchment, which had been sealed with the sigil of a warhammer atop a dwarfish rune. Adrik's heart leaped into his throat as he looked at the seal, his hands shook as he broke it and unfolded the parchment, and his blood went cold as he began to sift through the contents.

After reading the letter, the dwarf hurriedly packed his belongings, taking time to scrawl a note onto a scrap piece of parchment and slide it underneath Enna's door, confident that the combination of the travel and her arcane display would assure her slumber. He gathered his belongings and quickly exited the inn, placing them in his cart, hitching up his mules, and setting off. By sunrise the next day, Adrik Thornmallet was miles away from East Fellowdale.

Chapter 8

In a small room at the northwestern most point of the cottage on the outskirts of the Arcane University in Lohvast, Queen Merrian Arkalis knelt in front of a large burning candle atop a marble pedestal in the centre of the otherwise barren room. Her eyes were closed, focusing intently on the energy emanating from the candle. The ritual in which the Queen was engaging was not particularly complex, especially not when compared to some of the elaborate arcane rituals she had learned as a student at the university. Quite the contrary: the ritual was deceptively simple, though it was rarely used even by the few who knew it. It required little more than a fresh candle, a baseline knowledge of the infernal script, and a particularly high threshold for pain – all components which the Queen had in spades.

Sensing the flame of the candle reach its peak temperature, Queen Merrian, her eyes still closed, drew forth a small knife, its blade only a few inches long but razor-sharp nonetheless. Pressing the tip of the blade into her left palm, Merrian used all of her resolve to keep her hands steady and her eyes shut as she blindly, yet methodically, carved a symbol into her palm. The Queen was aided by the fact that the lines were already scarred into her hand, despite her best efforts to hide them. When she had completed the symbol, she stood and held her hand over the candle, careful not to let a single drop of the blood pooling within it fall.

"He who is the conqueror," she spoke in the infernal tongue. "Whose name is unspoken out of fearful reverence. He who controls all that is at home amid brimstone and flame. He who is controller of the weak and slayer of the lame, I call you forth, beckoning you to my realm from your own."

Upon completing the first half of the ritual, the Queen quickly overturned her palm, pressing her blood and the hand that cupped it down onto the flame. Fighting the searing pain, the Queen continued.

"Infernal Lord Nebalsus, I call you forth. I give you this body as a chamber for your voice. Come forth and speak!"

In an instant, the candle beneath the Queen's palm was snuffed, enveloping the small room in complete darkness. Merrian felt herself being sucked into her own consciousness, opening her mind's eye and seeing not the room in which she stood, but rather a large, terrible throne room. The walls, pillars, and floors looked to be some manner of obsidian, though upon closer examination would disprove this by virtue of the fact that the material pulsed in such a way that made them seem almost alive. Bas-reliefs of unspeakable acts carried out during countless wars, spanning centuries, continents, and even realms adorned the walls in a constant state of fluctuation, moving from one gruesome display to the next.

At the far end of the throne room sat a menacing throne made of the same material as the rest of the room, its form ever changing and contorting into countless unsettling shapes. The ethereal throne was occupied by a large, sinewy creature. It appeared to be roughly eight feet tall, and its body looked like that of a muscular human male whose skin had been flayed off as cleanly as a seasoned hunter might do to a hare. Its head looked like that of a wolf, though skinned in the same manner as the body. Although the face had a muzzle, no nose or mouth could be seen. Its eyes were blacker than the void of a starless night, but gleamed with terrifying intellect. As Merrian walked towards the being, it spoke.

"Why have you summoned me?" it bellowed. In spite of the fact that Nebalsus had no visible mouth, it had a voice, deep and menacing, that echoed through the throne room.

"I wish to bear news unto you," Merrian replied, a confident smirk on her face. "I now have total control over the Headmaster of Lohvast's arcane university."

"You believe this worthy of my summoning?" the demon growled, its glassy black eyes narrowing. "I expect news of great feats, of blood spilled in my name, of the signs that might herald my passage into your realm. Instead you bring me word that you have but a single arcane caster in your thrall?" Nebalsus' tone was even, but being that the demon was an embodiment of pure malice, there was an ever-present rage to its voice.

"Ever the narrow-minded one." Merrian shook her head, the smirk still present as she came within feet of Nebalsus' throne. "You fail to see the bigger picture, Lord."

"Impudence!" The demon raked its long, claw-like nails across one armrest. "I have conquered entire realms and held them within my grasp for aeons. You are an insignificant mortal with hold over but a fraction of a single mass of land. I have the power to annihilate your kingdom with a single word."

"And yet here you sit, a prisoner of your own realm," the Queen retorted. "I am not disputing your might, Lord, but you lack strategy. Else why would you be relegated to humouring this 'insignificant mortal' with a summoning ritual?" She leaned in close to the demon, feeling his intense heat emanating from his body. "Be assured, Lord, that your scion has the Mission well under her control."

Nebalsus' eyes burned into Merrian, his gaze one of seething hatred and utter resentment. It knew that it was unable to act, no more than a simulacrum within Merrian's mind. Finally, the demon slunk back into its throne, its eyes no less full of rage. "Speak of your progress."

"With pleasure," Merrian curtseyed low. "With Daylen Cresthill as my thrall, I will have access to hundreds of years worth of arcane literature, as well as nearly complete control over every arcane resource in Lohvast."

"Your methods confuse me, mortal. You know well that the Mission depends on the eradication of arcane power from your realm, yet your actions do nothing of the sort."

"Don't they?" Merrian raised an eyebrow. "We know that arcana bleeds into the mortal realm somehow, and yet we lack specifics. Access to the university's private well of knowledge may grant us clues as to where those wounds are, so that we might cauterize them."

"And what of this army of arcane casters that you amass?" The demon's face contorted into what one could constitute as a menacing grin. "You mean to round them up and have them executed?"

The Queen let forth a short, derisive laugh. "Nothing so idiotic."

"What is so idiotic about the completion of the Mission?!" the demon demanded. "You are ruler of your lands, so I demand you act as such!"

"Your shortsightedness amuses me to no end, Lord," the Queen grinned, beginning to stride back and forth in front of the throne. "When a ruler forces their hand, they breed dissent. This was Derrus Tyn's mistake. As it stands right now, I have a kingdom of citizens whom I have treated as people, not chattel. As such, I have bred genuine loyalty within them, so much so that they are willing to go to war on my very word! What good would it do me to eradicate hundreds of powerful arcane casters when I can have them cling to my words? These are men and women who I can utilize to fight for my cause," she paused and turned to face Nebalsus. "For our cause."

The demon's eyes narrowed knowingly, and it let out a deep, menacing laugh. "You are very wise, for a mortal. When I am ruler over all realms I shall grant you life eternal as my right hand."

"An honour I would graciously accept, Lord," the Queen responded as she bowed low once more.

Nebalsus raised a sinewy arm, making a shooing motion with his hand. "Go now, release my summon and commence your plan. Summon me forth once more when there is more news to be had."

"At once, Lord."

In an instant, the ritual was concluded, and Queen Merrian opened her eyes to the pitch darkness of the room, her hand throbbing in pain as she peeled the hardened wax and dried blood away from the scars that had been reopened and cauterized so many times before. The pain did not bother Merrian, though. It was a small price to pay for the greatness that she knew was right within her grasp.

Chapter 9

"What do you mean he's gone?!" O'doc Overhill paced back and forth in Enna Summerlark's room. Enna sat on her bed, looking numbly at the parchment she had found when she awoke.

"That's just it," she replied. "The note is so vague. All it says is, 'Dear friends, I regret that I must take leave on a matter of personal importance. Do not fret my well-being, I will return when I am able. Yours, Adrik Thornmallet.'"

"So, that seems fairly clear," Erasmus stated, leaning against the open door frame. "I'm sure it's nothing he'd want to worry us over."

"That's exactly what worries me," Enna responded, handing the parchment over to the half-elf. "Look at this note; the handwriting looks messy, rushed. If it were nothing important, Adrik would have waited until morning and given us a proper goodbye, not sneak out in the middle of the night. I think he knew we'd insist on going with him."

Erasmus took the note and read it carefully, dropping his hand to his side after finishing it. "Well, whatever the case is, the fact of the matter is that Adrik left and gave us no clues as to where he went."

"The barkeep?" O'doc offered.

Enna shook her head. "That was my first thought after I read the note when I woke up. He told me that people come and go at all hours, and that Adrik never stopped at the desk when he left."

"Wonderful." O'doc crossed his arms and leaned against the room's wardrobe. "How do we look for a dwarf that doesn't want to be found?"

"What about Professor Coldstone?" Enna perked up. "I've been reading up on divination spells in Varis' books. It's well beyond my abilities, but maybe..."

"We just met the man last night," Erasmus argued. "He made a kettle float for a few seconds, Enna, he's hardly an archmage."

"And do you know the Ghestal archmage personally?" Enna shot back "Or any other arcanists in the city, for that matter?"

The half-elf didn't respond, save for the glare he shot the young elf.

"What do you think, O'doc?" Enna turned to the halfling "You've known the professor longer than either of us, do you think he'd be capable of some kind of divination?"

O'doc shrugged. "It's worth asking. At this point, anything would help."

"Alright then, it's settled," Enna nodded, standing up and glaring back at Erasmus. "We're going to Professor Coldstone for help."

"Oh, hello." Professor Coldstone answered his door groggily, the hair on his head and the robe on his body equally unkempt. "I must say, I hadn't been expecting you until much later."

"I'm sorry if we're intruding, Professor," Enna smiled, trying not to appear too on-edge. "But we have a bit of a problem, and we need your help."

"A problem?" the professor repeated back. "What sort, my dear? Is everything alright?" He paused, looking the group over. "Where is your friend Adrik?"

"Well, that's the problem..." O'doc replied. "May we step in, Falken?"

Coldstone shook his head, as though to clear the morning fogginess from his mind. "Oh gods, my manners...of course, come in."

The companions followed the professor into his study, where he proceeded to clear piles of books and scrolls off several chairs, offering Enna, Erasmus, and O'doc a seat, opting himself to lean against a large oaken desk. "So," he began, looking each of the three over. "What exactly has happened?"

"Damned if any of us know," Erasmus replied, handing the professor the note. The half-elf had his misgivings about Coldstone but could not place them, and so, given the circumstances, had decided to put them aside for the sake of his friends.

"I found this note slid underneath my door this morning," Enna continued as the professor read over the parchment. "I don't understand it. He seemed fine last night, and this morning he was gone."

"The writing looks hectic..." Coldstone said, his eyes still affixed to the note. "I would love nothing more than to help, truly," He raised his gaze to meet Enna's, "but I'm not sure what I can do for you."

Enna's eyes dropped to the ground. "Oh... I just... I thought..."

"Falken," O'doc stood up and walked over to the professor. "I know you're not exactly the practicing arcanist you used to be, but Enna's been reading up on divination spells, scrying and whatnot. If there's any chance that you might know something that could help us find Adrik..."

The professor puzzled for a moment. After nodding thoughtfully, he stood up, and began to walk to the far end of the study. He leaned down and grasped the corner of a large, ornate rug that covered the study's floor. Pulling the rug back, the professor revealed a small trapdoor worked into the floorboards. "When I first came to East Fellowdale," he began as he started to work the trapdoor up, "the property on which we stand was much smaller. It belonged to an old historian whom I apprenticed under, and who later passed it on to me when he died. When I began my tenure at Ghest's arcane university, I began to add on to the property, try and make it mine, I suppose." Coldstone pulled away the trapdoor and placed it on the overturned section of rug, revealing a tight spiral staircase of wrought iron. "As it turns out, there was much the old man had kept from me."

Coldstone led the group down the cramped stairwell several tens of feet, before arriving at a small wooden door. The professor whispered something in elven and held out his wand, causing a bright light to emanate from the tip of the wand, illuminating the increasingly darkening area. Upon opening the door, the group was led into a large chamber shrouded completely in darkness. Unlike the subterranean prisons below Castle Rheth, there was no dank, musty smell. Rather, the chamber smelled of dust and disuse, more akin to an attic than a cellar. The professor rested his wand on a wall sconce, walking the perimeter of the chamber to light the torches sitting in the remaining sconces.

As Coldstone gradually brought a dim light to bear, the immenseness of the chamber was made apparent. Rows upon rows of tall bookshelves lined either side of the chamber, each one seemingly filled to capacity. Large, plain wooden tables with benches on either side sat amid the stacks, as the centre of the chamber acted as a corridor, with a simple wooden door placed at the end, opposite of the entrance. Upon completing his circuit, the professor led the group across the middle of the chamber toward the far door.

"What in the world is this place?" Enna asked, partially to herself, looking around as they walked.

"Being perfectly honest, my dear, I have no idea," the professor responded. "Many of the books are arcane tomes that I only wish I had the time to pore over, and many more are written in languages that I cannot even comprehend. Whether they are from beyond the Kingdoms, dead scripts from bygone eras, or something else entirely, I cannot tell."

The group reached the far side of the chamber, and Coldstone opened the door, revealing a smaller room just large enough to fit the four comfortably. In each corner of the room stood a small stone pillar topped with some manner of crystal, and in the centre sat two small daises.

"Well, this doesn't look menacing in the least," Erasmus commented offhandedly.

"It does seem dreary, I know," Coldstone conceded, "but there is something about this room that causes it to pulse with energy, I can feel it. If we are to try some manner of divination to locate your friend, this would be the place to do it."

"So what do you need?" O'doc asked.

"Well, this is the tricky part," the professor tapped his chin thoughtfully. "In order for me to properly scry someone's location, I'm going to need something connected to them. A lock of hair, a bit of clothing, something to that effect."

"Well that would have been good to know before you pulled us down into your little dungeon here," Erasmus responded, making no effort to mask his irritation. "Adrik took everything he had with him when he vanished."

"Not everything," Enna interjected, holding up her club and looking at the head. "Adrik gave this piece of quartz to me when I was a child."

Coldstone looked at the club thoughtfully. "It seems a bit of a long shot, but it might work." He took the club from Enna and placed it down between the two daises, then stepped up onto the dais nearest the door. "Enna my dear," the professor motioned to the unoccupied dais, "this spell will be a difficult task, and so I may require some assistance."

"How? My implement is lying on the floor, and I've never actually tried casting a divination spell."

"I will take care of the casting, Enna," Coldstone assured her. "I have yet to fully grasp it, but this room seems to be able to augment arcane power, like a glass lens used to focus on small objects. All I will need you to do is focus on Adrik when I begin scrying for him."

"Falken, are you sure this is a good idea?" O'doc asked. "Enna's still learning what her limits are. You saw what happened last night when she conjured a little fireball..."

"I cannot say with certainty that there aren't any risks involved," Coldstone admitted. "Most of what we are about to try I have never done, especially not in so great a scope."

"Why not have me give it a go, instead?" Erasmus asked. "I may only work with charming spells, but I'm more practiced than Enna."

"I'm not afraid," Enna said before the professor could answer. "If it's a matter of focusing on Adrik, I knew him before you did, Erasmus."

"Hardly. You met him once as a child before we met."

"It's still something, and by the sounds of it we're going to need every advantage we can get." Enna stepped onto the unoccupied dais and looked at Coldstone. "Go ahead, Professor, I'm ready."

The professor raised his hand and pointed it at the club on the floor. He spoke in Elvish.

"Kara sinte a' lye sina naug."

After a moment of absolute stillness, a soft light began to cover the small room, originating in the crystals atop each of the four pillars. As the light became more intense, a glow began to emerge from the quartz embedded in Enna's club. In a moment, the light from the pillars, as though it could no longer be contained, burst forth in bright beams all directed at the club. The beams continued to pour energy into the implement for several seconds before they extinguished, leaving the small room in darkness, save for the club, which was now pulsing with bright light and so much arcane energy that everyone in the room, even O'doc, felt it.

The light from the club began to pour upward, creating strange spectral images, too vague for anyone to ascertain.

"Now, Enna," Coldstone said, his eyes closed and his hand outstretched toward the light. "Concentrate on Adrik. Focus all your will toward locating your friend."

Enna nodded and closed her eyes, stretching one hand toward the light as she saw the professor do. She concentrated hard on the dwarf, picturing him traveling along on his wagon, one hand clutching the reigns of his mules while the other tried desperately to keep his ratty old tricorn hat from blowing away in the wind.

Wind...

Enna concentrated harder on the weather surrounding Adrik. The wind was cold and biting, and blowing in his face from the south.

Adrik was traveling south...

The strength of the wind meant there must not have been many trees or buildings to cause a natural windbreak. Open fields and a well-kept trade road opened up in Enna's mind's eye, and she could see her friend bracing against the wind as he soldiered his mules and wagon southbound, a scant few farms dotting the landscape, and a tremendous, expansive range of mountains in the southern horizon.

Enna tried focusing on the mountain range, to see if there was anything she could glean from it, when she noticed something begin to make its way into the foreground. It had started as a speck over the mountains, but quickly began to grow as it flew northbound, so quickly that Enna could not believe the thing's speed. As it came into Enna's focus, she gasped at the sight, as it appeared to be some manner of bear or cougar, but with the wings and head of an eagle. The fantastic beast swooped in ever closer, appearing to have some manner of rider on its back, when it suddenly changed its pitch, and dove down toward Adrik's cart, and showing no signs of slowing. Enna tried to cry out to her friend, despite being fully aware of the futility of doing so, and upon hearing her own voice in the fraction of a second before the beast reached Adrik, she fell abruptly into darkness.

Enna awoke to the feeling of a cool, damp cloth upon her forehead, and a soft purring in her ear. She opened her eyes, and as they came into focus she saw that she was still underground. She sat up, her neck stiff, and realized that she had been lain on one of the long tables in the large subterranean chamber. O'doc and Erasmus sat in nearby chairs, talking with Professor Coldstone, who sat on another of the tables and looked about as groggy as Enna felt.

"Oh, she's finally come to." O'doc looked over at the elf, the relief evident on his face. He, Erasmus, and Coldstone stood up and walked to her, the professor massaging his temples as they walked.

"What... happened?" Enna said finally. "How long was I out for?"

"Quite some time," Erasmus responded. "You and the Professor both."

"The sun's already begun to set." O'doc added. "We were starting to get worried, then Falken came to about half an hour or so before you did."

"That still doesn't really tell me what happened." Enna hopped off the table and dusted herself off. "I saw Adrik in his cart, riding toward a mountain range, then he was attacked by...."

"A gryphon," the Professor offered. "I would not have believed it myself, had I not seen it. I had thought gryphons were hunted into extinction centuries ago."

"So you saw it, too?" Enna asked.

"We all did," Erasmus responded. "It was like some kind of ghost image glowing up from your club. When you cried out, it flared up into nothing but a piercing light, and then you and the Professor both collapsed."

The cat that had been purring into Enna's ear stood up and walked across the table to her, nudging her hand with its head. Enna looked down at it, its sleek gray coat in stark contrast to its large yellow eyes, and began to pet it.

"I've been told Zarah here never left your side while you laid there," Coldstone smiled. "She must be quite fond of you. I have a hard time getting her inside for more than a few hours at a time."

"Zarah?" Erasmus noted. "Not many people give their cats Elven names. What inspired that choice?"

"Well, to call her 'my' cat would be something of a presumption," the Professor answered. "She simply showed up one day. I couldn't think of what to call her, so I began trying every name I came across in my studies. One might think me crazy, but I swear, the first time I called her Zarah, I could swear she looked at me like she was impressed that I had finally got it right." The Professor looked over at the cat and smiled before returning his gaze back to Enna. "Back to more pressing matters, however, I think I know where Adrik was in our vision."

"I'm fairly certain I know, too," O'doc added. "Northwest of Tillburg, taking one of the lesser used trade roads toward the Otharines."

"That was my guess," the Professor furrowed his brow. "He must have been riding straight through the night."

"What could possibly have made him do all this?" Enna asked, as much to herself as to her companions.

"I think it's pretty clear that that's a question we'll need to save for Adrik," Erasmus stated. "Only problem is, if what we all saw actually happened, we're going to need to get to the Otharines faster than any horse could take us." The half-elf looked down at O'doc and gave him a knowing glance. The halfling, lost in his own thoughts, was unaware of this until both Coldstone and Enna joined in.

"Why are you all..." O'doc began, his look of confusion quickly shifting to one of indignation. "No.

Not a chance. I know what you're all thinking. There has to be another way."

"If you can think of one, I'm sure we'd all be very interested in it," Erasmus retorted.

O'doc opened his mouth to try and protest, but quickly re-closed it, painfully aware of the fact that this was an argument that he was not going to win. The halfling closed his eyes and sighed, as if to brace himself for what he was about to say.

"Fine. First thing tomorrow morning, we set out north for Khalen Ridge."

Chapter 10

The sun poured through the stained glass windows of Daylen Cresthill's office, casting a colourful myriad of lights onto the headmaster's desk as he stared at the books stacked atop it. It had been nearly a week since Queen Merrian had left, and though Cresthill knew the Queen was nothing if not gracious about his rejection, he could not help but feel as though he had jilted her. The headmaster recounted their talk numerous times. His reasoning was sound, and she had conceded that fact to him. "A wise tactician," she had called him, adding that she would, indeed, return for a visit once all was said and done with Hallowspire.

Still, something ineffable about the conversation plagued the headmaster, so much so that the only way for him to put it from his mind was to throw himself into his work almost entirely. In the last week, the headmaster had began to scour the university's private libraries for every book, every scroll, every essay and dissertation that related in some way to the nature of arcana. The task was by no means an easy one, for as much as the people of the Four Kingdoms had used arcana for various reasons, there was little, if anything written about the true nature of it. The question of the source of arcane power had never been one that had bothered the headmaster to any worthwhile degree, and in truth, even his initial searches for answers in the past week had been born of little more than a passing curiosity. The more he searched through page after page and book after book, the less he found. He was constantly met with dead ends and unanswered questions, which bothered him beyond frustration, bordering on fury.

Five books sat upon Daylen Cresthill's desk. For all his scouring and sifting through the private library, all the headmaster was able to muster was five books. He walked over to the desk and picked up a page of parchment, reading over the notes he had written down on it. There were several references to the goddess Tymenthia, who struck a pact with the god Anduran to stave off beasts who had been attacking his children, the mortal races. Tymenthia brought the fae-folk from her kingdom, and instructed them to use her gift of arcana to drive back the threat. Impressed with the cooperation between the mortals and the fae-folk, Tymenthia granted the gift of arcana throughout the Four Kingdoms.

Cresthill shook his head. The myths were, of course, just that. Few people truly believed the old stories, and most only ever referenced them as parables or cautionary tales. Regardless, the myth was the closest thing the headmaster could find to an actual account of the origins of arcana, and knew that it had to be used as the starting point of his study, if only he could just find the sliver of fact within it.

"It's frustrating as all hells, isn't it?" A voice behind the headmaster spoke, causing him to turn on his heel, startled. Leaning against a tall bookshelf was a gaunt, sickly-looking halfling, casually inspecting his long fingernails.

The headmaster began to dash toward his nearby staff, hoping to cast a binding spell on the intruder. However, before he could reach the implement, he began to levitate, speeding past the headmaster and into the hands of the halfling. Before he could react, Cresthill felt his muscles seize, leaving him frozen in place.

"Tisk tisk, Headmaster Cresthill." The halfling strode over to face the headmaster, his jaundiced eyes glaring up at him. "Such unseemly manners. What is it with you book-learned arcanists, anyway? Someone slips in unannounced, and your first reaction is to try and cast some kind of spell on the person..." The halfling looked thoughtful for a moment. "I suppose I could stop sneaking about, but that's not really my prerogative."

"Who are you?" Cresthill gritted his teeth, fighting to speak.

"Lannister Ravenclaw," the halfling bowed, "at your service, at the behest of Queen Merrian."

Cresthill's eyes narrowed. "I don't believe you."

"Suit yourself." Lannister shrugged nonchalantly. "I was just sent here to check in on you, but feel free to send me away. I know you enjoy turning down things her Grace offers to you."

The headmaster was quiet a moment, trying to read the halfling. "Oh, by the gods," Lannister rolled his eyes, "you aren't going to be easy about this, are you?" With a snap of Lannister's fingers, the plush chair from the headmaster's desk slid over to its owner, causing the still-immobilized headmaster to be forced into a sitting position from which he could not move. Lannister walked closer to Cresthill, now looking the headmaster eye-to-eye. "Look, you're clearly better at reading books than you are people, so I am going to speak very slowly and explain everything to you. Queen Merrian, for reasons beyond my grasp, seems to care a great deal for you. When you turned down her offer of marriage, you didn't do a very good job of making it seem like you believed what you were saying. Her Grace told me to keep an eye on you and make sure you weren't planning on throwing your sorry ass off some cliff face in Frostpoint."

The halfling's argument caused Cresthill to take pause, yet he remained cautious. "Why am I only learning of this now? And how and why did you sneak into this room to reveal yourself?"

Lannister sighed, grabbing a nearby stool and pulling it to where he had been standing. "Queen Merrian was worried about discretion, didn't want you feeling emasculated. I happen to be the most discreet individual in her Grace's employ, so it only made sense that she'd ask me. I did as she asked, stayed quiet for a while, but the more I watched you just throw yourself so completely into your work, I felt awful for you."

"I don't need pity from some... rogue..." the headmaster sneered.

"First, my official title under her Grace is 'Security Expert,' so I'll thank you to respect that. Second, this isn't pity, it's sympathy. You aren't the only one who's had to forgo love for work, you know." Lannister leaned in, resting an elbow on the headmaster's knee. "Look, I can help you. I want to help you. You've got a hunch, and I've got sources that know how to find things."

"And what are you getting out of all of this?"

"I get to help a kindred spirit feel a bit better about himself," Lannister replied easily. "Plus, I tell her Grace that you're keeping well, and she rewards me for a job well done." The halfling waited for a moment, and when Cresthill did not respond, swept his arms out dramatically. "Come now, Headmaster, look at this room and think about the position in which you currently find yourself. If I was really some kind of filthy burglar, I could have paralyzed you, taken five items in here, and be living in luxury in Heavenguard before anyone even thought to check on you. Now, do you want my help with your little puzzle, or not?"

"It seems I only have one option in the matter, don't I?"

"Hardly. You say the word, and I'll be gone, as quiet as I arrived. The tricky bit is, you already let one life-altering proposition slip through your fingers. Can you refuse two in so short a span of time and still be able to live with yourself?"

The headmaster lowered his head as best as he was able, and let out a resigned, defeated huff. "Fine. Release me from this bind you've cast." With a wave of the halfling's hand, Cresthill felt his body slacken, collapsing into the chair's plush cushions. His muscles ached and his head throbbed, the former no doubt an aftereffect of the spell, and the latter out of sheer bewilderment. "I don't understand," he said, wincing as he stood up. "You were just able to bind me, move a piece of furniture, and dispel the whole thing without speaking a single command, not to mention the fact that I see nothing that might be your implement."

Lannister grinned and tossed the headmaster his staff, trying to ignore the searing sensation in his shoulder, a feeling that was present any time he used his recently acquired abilities. "I'm afraid I'll have to keep that my little secret for the time being. Let's just say that my abilities are a bit closer to the heart than your average arcanist." The halfling hopped off the stool and began to walk toward the headmaster's desk. "Now, what say you and I get started?"

ChapteR 11

The road to Khalen Ridge from East Fellowdale was narrow, winding, and treacherous, not at all as O'doc Overhill had remembered it.

"The trip ought to take less than a day." The halfling had told the group that morning as they packed the saddlebags on three horses and a pony that Professor Coldstone had loaned from a rancher just outside town. The Professor had insisted on accompanying the group, largely by virtue of the fact that there was a very good chance that they would encounter more dwarves than just Adrik in their attempt to locate him, and by that virtue it was not unwise to have someone who could speak some Dwarfish.

"I'm afraid that won't be the case, O'doc." Coldstone replied. "Unless of course I mistakenly took possession of a set of craftily disguised pegasi."

"What are you going on about, Falken? Back when I still lived at home, we'd be able to leave for East Fellowdale, run whatever errands needed to be run, and be back home in time for a late supper."

"It's been some years since you lived at home, O'doc," Coldstone retorted. "I've seen more of your family in the last ten years than you have: things have changed."

"Changed how? What's happened?"

"Well, it's really all a matter of Lord Graylock. In the last ten years, his two most infamous actions have been permanently disbanding the arcane university here, and striking a peace accord with the families of Majadrin. The former left your mother, like myself, largely out of work, and as such she took to really cultivating the Khalenese owl population, so much so that it's become the chief mode of transport among your family. As far as the latter, peacetime has meant fewer recruits for your father to train."

"Well then why wouldn't the old fool use the extra time to keep the roads in shape? It's not like he and my brother aren't able-bodied enough."

"He actually quite enjoys it, from what I'm told," Coldstone responded. "Claims that the rough roads keep anyone away who isn't serious enough to train under him."

"That sounds far too much like my father for me to try and dispute it," O'doc shook his head as he mounted the pony. "Alright, let's get this over with."

The roads just north of East Fellowdale were well-kept, and the coastal breeze kept the weather relatively temperate. By this late in the fall, Enna was normally accustomed to seeing frost coat the morning grass, so she was pleasantly surprised by the fact that, since the group had arrived along the coast, she hadn't yet needed to wear the extra furs she had packed when she left home. Two hours into the journey, however, much of the situation changed drastically. The road upon reaching Khalen Wood was all but terminated, changing into little more than a rough-hewn path littered with all manner of the fallen remnants of nearby trees. The path was so unfriendly that, just prior to entering the Wood, the group had stopped at a nearby farmstead to deposit their mounts, with the professor advising them that the remainder of the journey would be safer on foot.

The path within Khalen Wood had a gradual incline, and became more sparse and erratic as it progressed. The wind eventually changed directions, originating from the north, and bringing with it a biting chill that caused the entire group to bundle up heavily. Indisputably the greatest change in scenery, however, were the trees of Khalen Wood. The foliage seemed to grow exponentially the further in and further up the group traveled, with oaks so wide around it that it would have taken eight to ten full-grown humans, arms stretched out, to form a perimeter around the trunk. Pine cones the size of Enna's head dotted the ground, the tops of the trees from which they had fallen poking out tens of metres above a forest canopy that was already at least twice as tall as anywhere else in the Four Kingdoms.

"This is incredible..." Erasmus said, nearly catching his foot on an errant root as he took in the view overhead. "I've heard stories, but I've never actually seen Khalen Wood. It's even more immense than I imagined."

"You think it's big for you, try being my size," O'doc smirked in spite of himself. As much as he dreaded the prospect of returning to the Wood, he could not help but admit, at least to himself, that it felt good being so close to home.

"It is beautiful, O'doc," Enna found herself gazing toward the immense canopy as well, gasping suddenly as she spotted a large, shadowed form overhead. She reached forward and grabbed Professor Coldstone's arm, pointing in order to draw his attention overhead. "Professor, look! Is that..."

"I'm afraid not, my dear," Coldstone smiled. "Just a nest."

"Most of the Khalenese owls should be hunkering down for winter by now," O'doc added. "I doubt we'll see many at all."

"I'd not speak too soon if I were you," Erasmus told the halfling, gesturing north and upward with his eyes at a large white form floating in the distance. The creature moved majestically through the air, sailing effortlessly through the large branches overhead. The owl's size was not lost on any of the companions, only becoming more impressive as it came closer. It did not take long for the group to notice that the owl was not alone, but was instead carrying what appeared to be another halfling on some manner of harness on its belly. The owl glided in low, landing roughly fifty feet from where the group stood. The halfling rider untied herself from her harness and began to walk toward the group with purpose, holding her long blue robes up so as to avoid catching them on the assorted foliage.

O'doc swallowed nervously, and walked forward to greet the rider, putting on the most convincing smile he could muster. "Odonwa!" he called out as they neared one another. "How's my favourite older sister?"

The halfling's question was met with a slap directly across the face, and a smoldering expression. "O'doc Honeytongue Overhill..." his sister fumed, her fists clenched at either side. "I've got half a mind to beat some sense into that head of yours! Do you have any idea how long it's been?"

"Not long enough to receive a more cordial welcome, apparently," O'doc rubbed his reddened cheek.

"It's almost been eleven years!" Odonwa cried. "Do you have any idea what that's been like for everyone? Not knowing where in the Kingdoms you're gallivanting around from one day to the next? Not knowing whether you're alive or dead in some ditch, save for what we hear from Aunt Caliope every six months?"

"Odonwa, I..." O'doc fumbled, trying to collect his thoughts. "Look, now's not the time... My friends and I...we need your help."

"Oh, what happened? Do you have some nefarious debt to pay?" Odonwa asked, looking over her brother's shoulder at his companions. "Falken? What are you doing here? Can you please tell me what sort of trouble this one's got himself into?"

"I can vouch for your brother, Odonwa, this is trouble not of his making." The Professor stepped forward, followed by Erasmus and Enna. "This is Erasmus Stonehand and Enna Summerlark, friends of O'doc who came to me the other night in East Fellowdale looking for some help. They had another companion, a dwarf named Adrik Thornmallet, who vanished two days ago with little more than a hurried note. We fear he traveled toward the Otharines, and that he may need help."

Enna stepped forward and curtsied. "Your brother has told me much about you and your family. It's a pleasure to finally meet another Overhill, although I'm sorry about the circumstances."

"The pleasure is mine," Odonwa walked over to the elf and smiled, returning the bow. "I'm glad to see my brother isn't associating himself with complete riff-raff."

"O'doc has been nothing if not a gentleman since we've met," Enna looked at her friend knowingly, and he smiled back at her, evidently relieved that she omitted the rocky start the two had when they met.

Odonwa turned around and looked at her brother, nodding approvingly. "Well well, little brother, who would have thought you'd grow up when you grew up?"

"What's that supposed to mean?" O'doc smiled back. With the initial awkwardness of seeing his sister past him, the halfling was beginning to feel surprisingly comfortable with the situation.

"You were a complete terror as a boy," Odonwa turned back to her brother's friends. "And he always managed to weasel his way out of getting into any trouble. It's how he got his middle name."

"I'll happily take Honeytongue over Lightningball any day," O'doc teased.

"Don't get jealous because I was named after my first arcane spell."

"A lucky coincidence on your part," O'doc laughed. "Mother and Father gave you that name because of your quick-flash temper, and the fact that people are afraid they might be struck." The halfling pointed to his still-reddened cheek to emphasize his point.

The two halflings laughed with camaraderie only shared among siblings. "I've missed you, you little terror." Odonwa opened her arms and pulled O'doc into a tight embrace that he gladly reciprocated. "All of us have missed you."

"I've missed you all, too." O'doc replied genuinely, feeling a weight lift from him as he spoke. "Where is everyone else?"

"Mother and Father left for Hallowspire a few weeks ago, something about King Renton looking for a new Archmage. Mother jumped at the opportunity to visit Rheth for the first time since all that unsanctioned arcana nonsense."

"And what about O'den and Odessa?"

Odonwa stared at her brother blankly, as though she could not understand the nature of his question. "O'den and Odessa both left Khalen Ridge years ago. O'den moved to Tillburg and became captain of King Meklan's royal guards, and Odessa fell in love with a young Gnomish trapper who came to train under Father some years ago. They married a year ago, and they live in a cabin they built themselves northwest of here."

"Odessa's married?!" O'doc gasped. "How? She's so young!"

"Is she? Odessa's only three years your junior, O'doc. She may have been a child when you left, but..."

Odonwa didn't continue her sentence. She didn't need to. The gravity of the situation was beginning to weigh heavily on O'doc. Odessa may have been a child when he left, but now she was a woman. His family and his home had grown and changed while he was gone, and he missed it. O'doc's head hung as he allowed the reality of his actions to sink in. "I'm sorry I missed the wedding..."

"So were we," Odonwa smiled weakly before taking a deep breath and steeling herself. "But what's done is done, and you said you needed help."

The group, led by Odonwa, walked for nearly another two hours, ascending through Khalen Wood mostly in silence. O'doc's sister happily agreed to letting the companions take four owls to the Otharines, but the bittersweetness of the reunion of the two Overhills still hung thick in the air, making extensive conversation among the group a difficult task. Eventually, they came across a large, flat clearing in the Wood, largely featureless save for a number of large rocks resting in a semicircle on the far side of the clearing.

"You'll all have to excuse me," Odonwa said, turning around to face the rest as they approached the rocks. "We use a charm spell to keep control over the owls for flight. It's been passed down to every Overhill arcanist for five generations, but I'm still working on the nuances of it." She turned back around and stepped forward, drawing a small crystalline orb from her robes, closing her eyes and concentrating. After taking a few deep breaths, she began to speak the spell in a monastic drone.

"Noldo dulin 'en 'I taur, lasta 'a nin peth, lasta 'a nin naia."

Odonwa repeated the spell several times, each time hearing nothing but her own voice, but repeated the words nonetheless. The halfling was so focused on the spell that she barely noticed when a second voice joined in reciting the spell, a deeper voice that sung the words in a raspy tenor, rather than speaking them. The voice was accompanied by the soft plucking of some kind of strings. Unbeknownst to Odonwa, she had begun to match the tone of her own voice to that of the voice aiding her, until she, too, was singing. Finally, after several minutes, she could hear the distant beating of wings. Opening her eyes and looking upward, she saw several Khalenese owls, their feathers white in preparation for the oncoming winter. Looking to her side, Odonwa saw that the voice that aided her had belonged to Erasmus Stonehand. He looked back at her and shrugged.

"Charms are something of a specialty of mine," he said with a smirk. Caliope had told Odonwa and her family of Erasmus when she gave them news about O'doc, and Odonwa had always pegged the bard as a bit of a shady individual. The fact that he looked the part of a scruffy sell-sword when they finally met didn't help to assuage her apprehension, but as she looked at the half-elf now, she felt that perhaps he wasn't quite the selfish rogue she had painted him out to be.

The owls glided down and perched themselves on the rocks, looking expectantly at the companions. Odonwa walked toward the central bird and began to caress its feathered breast, the bird letting out a soft, contented mewing hoot in response. "Falken, to the left edge of this clearing is a wooden and stonework rack with harnesses. Would you please gather four of them?"

The professor did so, and with help from Odonwa and O'doc, the owls were soon rigged for travel. "I almost can't remember what it's like traveling by owl," O'doc smiled as his sister helped him into his own harness.

"It's the same as it ever was," Odonwa smiled back. "Pull the reigns left or right to steer, use your legs to control your pitch."

"We'll take good care of them, Odonwa," Enna called out, looking over at the halfling. "Thank you for everything. I hope to meet the rest of your family when we return."

"As do I," Odonwa bowed, then turned back to her brother. "O'doc, I'm sorry about earlier, I was..." she looked at the ground and began to fidget with her hands.

"It's nothing to be sorry for," O'doc replied, a lump beginning to form in his throat. "Look, I... there are things I've done that you, that everyone, would likely not think kindly of, and people that..." he took a deep breath, trying to maintain his composure. "What I'm trying to say is, there are reasons why things have been the way they've been, but not for the reasons you may think, and I'd be lying if I said that I wasn't full of regret about it."

Odonwa looked at her brother, forcing a smile as she blinked away tears. "Just don't be such a stranger anymore, okay? You bring those owls back safely, and maybe come for a proper visit."

"I will," O'doc nodded, and his sister backed away as the he and his companions cracked the reigns on the owls and took flight.

As O'doc watched his sister wave as she shrunk from sight, he came to the realization that he had just, for the second time in his life, left his home without properly saying goodbye. The halfling made a silent promise to himself that he would return to Khalen Ridge, his home, as soon as possible, and would not make the mistake a third time.

ChapTeR 12

Travel by Khalenese owl, as Enna quickly realized, was incredibly fast. O'doc led the pack, evidently so exhilarated by the feeling of riding an owl for the first time in years that the elf noticed that he could not help but let out the occasional holler of excitement, though barely audible to Enna over the beating of the owls' wings. The sun had only just begun to descend from its apex when the companions left Khalen Wood, and had just begun to hang low over the Windswept Sea as the Otharines came into view.

Enna particularly marveled over the sight of the oranges, reds, and magentas as they bled out into the sea, making it look as though it was set aflame. Her silent contemplation was broken, however, by the alarmed calls of her owl, as well as those of her friends.

Looking forward, the elf saw O'doc and his owl quickly dip, narrowly avoiding some manner of spear being hurled toward them. As O'doc dropped from sight, the attacker became apparent to Enna, as in the distance she could see a gryphon hurling itself toward her. On the beast's back rode what appeared to be a dwarf in full plate armour, holding the gryphon's rein in one hand, and reaching for another spear with the other. Unexpectedly pulling back on the reins of her own winged mount, Enna felt the owl right itself, its belly exposed as much as Enna was, to the attacker.

The owl began to beat its wings upwards, causing the dwarf to adjust its aim accordingly. Enna seized the opportunity to reach down and grab her club, trying to maintain control of her owl with only one hand. As the dwarf loosed its spear, Enna pointed her club and concentrated on the missile. Calling out an elvish command that she could barely hear herself, the elf felt a surge of energy course through her body, manifesting as a bright ball of orange flame that burst forth from the club head, striking the spear mid-flight, and causing it to spiral out of control and plummet toward the ground, a trail of smoke marking its descent.

A sudden cold began to spread through Enna's body, in spite of the soft down of the owl along her back. The chill weakened her, though the rush of the moment kept her alert enough to notice her owl letting out a cry, the bird's flight pattern going awry for a moment before it began to fly on its original course southward toward the Otharines. Enna shook her head to clear it, realizing that, though she was traveling in the direction she wanted, she did not will the owl to return along this path. In fact, as Enna looked ahead of her, she saw the gryphon with the dwarf rider whose spear she had deflected. The gryphon was flying toward the mountain range as well, but not with the haste of egress. Enna tugged at the reins of her owl, but to no avail, as the bird methodically followed the gryphon, as if under some manner of charm more powerful than what was cast by Erasmus and Odonwa. Looking to her left and to her right, Enna could see her companions' owls, flying with the same unnatural rhythm of her own. Looking down, the elf could see how high they all flew above the ground, and quickly dismissed any notion of she and her friends cutting themselves from their harnesses. The four companions were trapped for as long as the dwarf ahead of them saw fit, and in the disdain of this realization, and the lingering weakness from having cast her spell just moments earlier, Enna allowed her eyes to flutter closed as she and her friends glided helplessly to their fate.

Enna was roused back into consciousness by the jerking feeling of her owl touching down on solid ground. The chill that filled the elf from the inside was gone, replaced by the biting chill of strong, wintery winds. Night had begun to envelope as the snow covering the ground was reflected by the pale light of the moon in the clear sky. It did not take long for Enna to realize that she and her friends had arrived amid the vast expanses of the Otharine Mountains. Her observation was cut short by the point of a halberd being waved in her face. The polearm was held by a dwarf in armour similar to what the one riding the gryphon had been wearing.

"You, elf!" the dwarf grunted through his relatively short beard. "Loose yourself from that bird. No funny stuff, or you and your friends all get skewered."

Enna did as she was commanded, relieved if only by the fact that her captor had just insinuated that her friends were safe. The dwarf, who looked surprisingly young to Enna up close, took her hands and bound them behind her back. Another dwarf, a female, and one of many that looked as though they had been standing in a large circle around the landing area, stepped forward and searched the owl's harness, and removed all Enna's possessions from it, proceeding then to search Enna herself, taking Enna's club and putting it with the rest of the belongings. With a prodding from the first dwarf, Enna began to march forward, toward what looked like a stone and metalwork platform, enclosed by an iron cage that was suspended by a thick rope.

As she approached the cage, Enna could not help but smile as she saw Erasmus, O'doc, and Professor Coldstone, though the three of them were being marched toward the platform in a similar manner. None of the companions dared more than a relieved smile and a sidelong glance at the others, however, fearing the implications of any sudden movement or sound. The four were all marched to the platform and goaded inside, the iron door shut and locked behind them.

"Well," Erasmus broke the silence as the platform began to slowly descend down the large pit that the platform evidently hung above, "this is certainly a fine mess you've gotten us into, Coldstone."

"I beg your pardon? I'm not sure I understand how this predicament is my doing."

"Oh, really?" the condescension in the bard's voice was thick. "You think these dwarves would have noticed our approach so easily had we not been flying on damned giant owls?"

"We all agreed that the owls would be the fastest way to travel," Enna interjected.

"Well maybe if the professor here were as great a mind as you all seem to think, he'd have come up with a better idea."

"That's not fair, Erasmus," Enna chided her friend. "Professor Coldstone has done nothing but help us."

"Help us into a wrought iron cage being lowered into a dank hole!" Erasmus snapped back. "I don't understand why you keep defending him."

"Maybe because she's got enough wit to know better than to trust the jealous accusations of a scruffy sell-sword with a pretty voice." Professor Coldstone retorted, glaring at Erasmus for a moment before the half-elf tried, in spite of both his bindings and the lack of space within the cage, to lunge at the Professor. O'doc and Enna threw themselves at Erasmus and managed to subdue him, but not before his dark brown eyes bored a look of utter contempt straight through the Professor's glare, causing the arcanist to stand down.

"What in the hells is the matter with you?!" Enna looked at Erasmus, who would not meet her eyes, and then to Coldstone, who looked away and let out a resigned huff. "Both of you! We are trying to find Adrik, and we won't be able to do a very good job of it if O'doc and I have to watch over the two of you as though you were a pair of bickering cats. I don't know what sort of problems the two of you have with one another, nor do I care at this particular moment, so keep them at arm's length until we get back to East Fellowdale, understood?"

Neither the bard nor the Professor said a single word for the remainder of the descent. Indeed, not one of the companions spoke for a long while as they were slowly lowered past the walls of stone that were dimly lit by some manner of glowing rings of light that wrapped intermittently down the cylindrical shaft, which gave off a soft green glow.

Finally, the platform halted, having hit firm ground, and the companions were ushered out by two more dwarves, armoured like the others, but wielding short swords rather than polearms. The long corridor into which the group was led was evidently carved into the mountain, yet rather than looking like a mineshaft, dark, dank, and roughshod, the walls of the corridor were smooth as polished wood, and along the walls and ceiling were strips that glowed in a similar fashion to the rings of light during the group's descent. The corridor's ceiling was low, so much so that all but the dwarves and O'doc needed to crouch slightly as they walked through it. The Professor, his face so near the strips of soft light, was able to notice that they were strips of metal, inlaid with writing that he was unable to discern, as even the slightest pause in his forward march was met with the prodding blade of one of the dwarves.

The companions twisted and turned down a number of corridors similar to the first, many decorated with ornate bas-reliefs or woven tapestries that the companions were marched past without an opportunity to really look at them. They made their way through innumerable doors and passed some stonework and metalwork until none but the dwarves had the faintest idea of their direction. Finally, they arrived at a heavy stonework door, which led to a small room with six small pallet beds, and a large clay pot in one corner, presumably for relieving oneself. One by one, O'doc, Erasmus, Enna, and Professor Coldstone were pushed into the chamber, and the stonework door closed behind them.

The companions waited, uncertain as to how long they had been there. O'doc laid on one of the hard, uncomfortable pallet beds, tossing and turning before eventually falling asleep. Erasmus laid on one of the beds as well, his legs from knee down hanging from the foot of it as he stared at the ceiling, seemingly deep in thought. The Professor sat on the side of one bed, attempting to study one of the light strips at length, though his eyes and mind were heavily weighted by the day's events. Enna curled up on another of the beds, covering herself with her cloak as a makeshift blanket. Clasping her golden ear cuffs in one hand, the elf fought. She fought the tears of despair welling up in her eyes, she fought the encroaching fear of Adrik's well-being, she fought the homesickness that sometimes ate away at her from the pit of her stomach, and she fought the sleep that she knew would only be a brief, restless reprieve from the situation in which she presently found herself. Finally, after a long while, she lost the final fight, and drifted off into that reprieve.

The whole group awoke to the sound of the large stone door opening in front of them. Two dwarves, different from the ones that brought them to the cell, entered and began to pull the companions to their feet, and shuffled them back out the door. Standing at the opposite side of the corridor was a female dwarf in plate armour. She had no helmet on, allowing her ornately-braided red and silver hair to flow freely. Her face, aged and scarred, was sharp but not unattractive, while her red-brown eyes, while not malicious, glared at the companions with intensity. She turned to one of the guards and said something to him in Dwarfish, to which the guard nodded in response. Acknowledging this, the female dwarf looked the group over before motioning for the guards to follow her with the companions as she began to stride down the halls.

"What did she say?" Enna asked the Professor in a whisper as they made their way through more labyrinthine stonework hallways.

"Something about the thane and an audience, I think?" Coldstone whispered back, not entirely able to make out the dialect.

"Silence!" the female dwarf cried out as she led. "I can speak the northern trade tongue, so do not think that you can make me a fool by speaking it in my presence."

"Where are you taking us?" O'doc asked.

"His Lordship Thane Morabendar wishes to look upon the three mysterious northerners who invaded his airspace last night," the dwarf responded without looking back. "What he does from there is anyone's guess."

No one made any effort to get any more information out of the dwarf, all realizing the futility of the task. Instead, the companions marched along in silence until they arrived at a large pair of stonework doors inlaid with ornate metalwork. The female dwarf motioned to the two guards, each of whom took a handle and began to pull the doors open. The female dwarf then walked through the doors, motioning for the companions to enter, following her into what appeared to be a large throne room.

"Kneel before the Thane," she commanded as she led them within a few yards of the throne. The group obliged, and the dwarf continued walking, saying something to Thane Morabendar in Dwarfish.

"Merida!" the thane cried out in a voice that was all too familiar to the companions. "Release these people from their bindings! These are not invaders, but friends of clan Thornmallet!" The friends then lifted their eyes to see the thane striding down from his throne toward them, and that Thane Morabendar was, in fact, Adrik Thornmallet.

Chapter 13

The War Mages of Lohvast were a force spoken of, and oftentimes sung about, throughout the Four Kingdoms. Their craft had become largely ceremonial, as the Kingdoms had been in a state of relative peace for nearly two centuries, but it was practiced nonetheless for a number of reasons. Despite the fact that there was no difference between the arcana used by the War Mages and any other arcanist, there was a sort of pageantry that one only ever finds among those with military training, so that even the most basic drills carried out by the mages were a sight to behold, and oftentimes the subject of spectacle during festivals in Heavenguard.

Archmage Elbar looked down into the arcane barracks in Heavenguard, looking at the War Mages with all the wonder of the children who gawked at them in the streets during High Summer, and the reverence of a fellow arcanist. Elbar's father had wanted him to become a War Mage, as he had been, but the young Elbar, having only ever seen the War Mages in peacetime, balked at the notion, seeing them as little more than aggrandized jesters and acrobats, who threw the gift of arcana away on petty displays recycled year after year, festival after festival. Elbar had thought it much more the noble pursuit to serve the kingdom more directly, working his way through the hierarchy of arcane bureaucracy, from providing protection to mercantile houses, to advising middling lords, finding himself now as the right hand to Queen Merrian herself, and arbiter of all arcane activity in Lohvast.

Or so the archmage had thought when he initially ascended to the position. It had become apparent during his tenure, however, that the queen did not need Elbar. She was, herself, a gifted arcanist, as had been the whole of the Arkalis bloodline. Most of the tasks Elbar had been relegated to, the formal appointment of other arcanists to noble houses and the like, was largely ceremonial, pageantry that the Queen was either too busy to see to herself, or was ceremonially undertaken by the archmage. In recent months, it seemed that the Queen had begun to eschew Elbar's advice altogether, opting for the council of that halfling that had recently come into the fold, her "security adviser" or some other inane title added purely as a formality.

And so, Archmage Elbar looked upon the drilling War Mages and let out a resigned sigh. The irony was not lost on him: He had viewed War Magery as useless pageantry, worked all his life to reach a position where he believed himself to able to serve Lohvast with maximum efficacy, and now on the eve of an actual war, he wanted nothing more than to shirk whatever ceremonial pomp for which he had been scheduled and join the men and women he saw below and serve his kingdom, rather than merely act as a servant of it.

"Such a spectacle, isn't it, Archmage Elbar?" Queen Merrian caught the Archmage unaware as she approached him, causing the small man to nearly leap into the air as he straightened his posture and smoothed the folds of his robes.

"Apologies, your Grace," Elbar stammered, bowing his head low. "I was caught in a moment of childish enthrallment. It won't happen again."

"Oh, don't grovel, Elbar," the Queen rolled her eyes. "You've every reason to want a front-row seat to such a sight."

Queen Merrian turned and motioned to the training ground below, where a group of War Mages, roughly twenty or thirty, stood in two lines shoulder to shoulder. The commanding arcanist in back of the lines called out a command, and the first line knelt down, pressing their hands to the ground in a flourish. As if rising up from the ground itself, a thick fog began to emanate from where the War Mages knelt, quickly shrouding the entire training ground. Nothing could be seen from the Queen and Archmage's vantage point but the fog, and shortly after there came a second command, and all at once bright bolts of lightning began to illuminate the fog, revealing the silhouetted forms of the War Mages within it. The lightning continued in a dazzling display for several moments until the fog eventually dissipated, revealing the War Mages below, as well as the blackened remains of roughly thirty wooden dummies on the end of the training ground opposite them. The smoking wooden remains were in stark contrast to the wall behind them, however, which remained unblemished.

"I'd love to see those Hallowspiran simpletons stand up to that," Queen Merrian smirked satisfactorily. "A pity I won't be able to see our swift victory unfold first-hand." She looked over to the Archmage. "What do you think, Elbar?"

"It is truly an incredible sight," Elbar remarked, still transfixed on the training below. "Now, to truly understand the implications of what the War Mages are capable of, your Grace I can think of no nobler a way to serve the kingdom."

"You find your position as Archmage... unfulfilling?" the Queen's voice was calm and inquisitive.

"Oh... No, your Grace, of course not..." Elbar stammered. "I meant no disrespect to my station, I only..."

"No no, I understand," the Queen smiled, raising a hand to stay the Archmage's explanation. "Below us are men and women who have not only achieved complete mastery over arcana, but are willing to lay down their lives to uphold the values that allowed them that opportunity. It is truly admirable."

"Your Grace..." The Archmage swallowed hard, his eyes down and his face beginning to feel flushed. "I was never trained in the matters of war, but I wish you to know that, as Archmage of Lohvast, I willingly avail myself to this war in whatever means you see fit. Though I am not a War Mage, I wish you to know that I am not unwilling to sacrifice my well-being, as long as it is in service of this kingdom."

The Queen placed her hand on the Archmage's shoulder, and he looked up to see her smiling at him. "Tavon, you are a good man. In the histories of the Four Kingdoms, I've no doubt that you will be remembered, especially among all the Archmages." The Queen looked deep into the Archmage's eyes, and began to say something else. He could not understand what was being said, however, as it seemed to be in a language he could not comprehend.

Suddenly, a haze began to descend on Elbar's mind, causing him to feel as though he were in a dream. He saw Queen Merrian turn and walk away, beckoning him to follow. He did so, but in his current state was unable to tell whether or not the action was of his own volition. He followed the Queen down an ornate set of stairs at the end of the balcony they had been on, down into the halls of the barracks. The building did not have a complex layout, offering little more than sleeping quarters, a cookery and mess hall, a large public library in which the War Mages could study, and a small number of private studies for those with higher rank. The Queen approached what should have been the door to the library, but it was unmarked save for a strange sigil that the Archmage did not recognize.

The Queen entered and the Archmage followed into what indeed looked like a library, but with ceilings so high that they could not possibly exist within the confines of the barracks building. Robed figures sat amid the numerous tables that lined the central aisle of the room, but they were all hooded, and did not bear the colours of Lohvast. Elbar recognized none of this, however, and simply followed Queen Merrian in his dreamlike haze. At the centre of the library sat a stone dais, onto which the Queen led the Archmage, turning him about-face and draping upon him and herself with a pair of cloaks that were similar to the crimson robes being worn by those at the tables. Without any prompting, the robed figures all stood up from their seats and gathered around the dais, raising their heads up, though their hoods still largely shrouded their faces.

Queen Merrian leaned into the him and whispered, "You are about to serve your kingdom, and your queen, in a manner that you could not in your grandest dreams have ever fathomed. Are you prepared, Archmage Elbar?"

The Archmage nodded slowly. His mind and body still seemed in a fog, and the Queen's whisper, despite being right at his ear, sounded as though it were leagues away and echoing off cold stone, but he heard what she had said, and knew that his consent was his own. This was to be the Archmage's crowning achievement in his tenure that he might prove instrumental in ensuring that the unenlightened menace of Hallowspire would be dealt with quickly. He could faintly hear the Queen speaking and the hooded figures answering her in unison, but he could not understand what they were saying. He was not sure if this was an effect of his haziness, or if those around him were speaking a tongue he could not understand. It hardly mattered to the Archmage, whose thoughts were on the accolades he would receive, the songs that sung of his deeds, and the pages chronicling his role in the Great Arcane War. A smile spread across his face, unhindered by the figure of Queen Merrian walking out in front of him. His eyes and mind were so clouded that he did not see the Queen draw forth a gilded goblet and large, ornate dagger. His thoughts were so far from his body that he was numb to the feeling of the cold blade plunging deep into his belly, of the warm blood flowing out of him and into the goblet. In his final moments, Archmage Tavon Elbar remained smiling, thinking only of how he was finally serving his kingdom, his Queen, and her mission.

Chapter 14

Tucked well into the bosom of the easternmost stretch of the Otharine mountains, carved into immense caves both natural and manufactured well below the bases of the numerous summits, was the city of Deltharduin, capital city of the Morabendar thaneship. Amid the pristine, twisting halls and corridors that made up the city was Citadel Moraben, ancestral home of Clan Thornmallet. On any given evening, the Thane of Morabendar could be found dining in the citadel's great hall among close friends and other dwarves of prominence within the city. On this night, however, the Thane was nowhere to be seen in the great hall, nor was the commander of the Morabendine army. Presently, in a smaller, more private chamber further into the heart of Citadel Moraben, Thane Morabendar, known to his friends as Adrik Thornmallet, sat down to supper at a small stone table surrounded by the people he trusted most: his friends from the north, Enna, O'doc, Erasmus, and the Professor, and his sister, Merida Mettlehelm, commander of the Morabendine army. Despite the intimate setting and trusted group, however, all in the room were eating little, and saying even less.

"Friends, sister..." Adrik looked sympathetically around the table at everyone seated there. "The last day or two have been a trying time for you all, I'm sure. You must all have developed the most voracious of appetites by now. I bid you, please, eat!"

"Is that an order from his Grace Thane Morabendar?" Erasmus glared across the table at the dwarf, the incredulity in his voice so thick it hung over the stonework table.

"Watch that mouth of yours, fairy-bastard," Merida shot back at the bard. "If not for Adrik stepping in on your behalf, a choice I don't entirely agree with," she looked sidelong at her brother before returning her eyes to Erasmus, "I'd have seen you strung up by your own lute strings."

"Caster's a mandolin."

"Oh, I beg your pardon. When I was taught sixty-eight different ways to kill a man, they never mentioned boring a person to death explaining the difference."

"Sixty-eight?" Erasmus nodded in mock-admiration. "I'm marveled that you can count that high."

"Enough!" Adrik bellowed. His voice took on a deep, commanding quality that none but Merida had ever heard from him before, and caused the bickering parties to take pause, and all in the room to direct their attention to the dwarf. He looked stern a moment, looking back and forth between Erasmus and Merida. Convinced that neither was going to continue to prod the other, he slumped back into his chair, as though that single show of authority had drained him.

"Adrik," O'doc looked across the table at his friend, "why didn't you tell us where you were going, or about any of this?"

The dwarf shook his head slowly, a solemn smile forming at the side of his mouth as he stared right past the halfling. "For fear that a situation very near to this would play out as a result, friend."

"You still haven't told us why you left so suddenly," Enna mentioned.

"Nor does he have any obligation to," Merida muttered.

"Sister, enough!" Adrik spoke to her in Dwarfish. "Intentional or no, these are guests."

"Being north so long has made you soft, brother," Merida replied in kind. "You've even begun to speak with their accent. They've no business in Deltharduin."

"They could be assets, Merida. They will be willing to help, I know."

"Fine." Merida stood up and began to walk toward the door. "You are Thane, do as you like, but by Othar, Uthar, and Mirandira, I'll not be putting any soft-skinned northerners in my ranks." She marched out of the room, closing the stonework door behind her with a slam.

Adrik turned his attention to Erasmus, the annoyance evident on his face. "Erasmus, I will have you know that that was the Commander of the Morabendine army, Lady Merida Mettlehelm. I'll thank you to speak to her with more respect."

"To what end, Adrik? So she can berate the lot of us some more? You've no problem with us speaking plainly to you, and you're a damned dwarven Thane, why should I care what that miserable crone's title is?"

"Because that 'miserable crone' is my sister." Adrik's words were terse and frustrated, edging on anger. "Othar's beard, Erasmus, what has gotten into you?"

"What's gotten into me?" the bard let out a short laugh. "You make your grand speeches about helping us, helping Enna, and then you up and vanish without so much as a proper goodbye, right as we're about to maybe make some progress. Not only that, but we all drop what we're doing to track you down, worried that you were in trouble..."

"I never asked for you to seek me."

"We nearly get ourselves killed, Adrik, by some of your cavalry! And the best part of it all? We go through all that to help our trouble-stricken friend, only to find out that he's not who he claims, and has been living in the lap of luxury since he left. You'll have to excuse me if I'm not in the cheeriest of moods." Erasmus stood up and began to walk toward the exit "I'm afraid I'm not terribly hungry, *your Grace*, I think I'll retire for the night." The bard left the room with less clamor than Merida had earlier, but with no less indignation. Adrik sat back in his large chair, deflated, a deep pondering look on his face.

"Don't let Erasmus bother you too much," O'doc offered. "Every now and again he has his moments. I'll speak with him later, try and get his head seeing straight."

"In all fairness to Erasmus, though," Enna added, "he was right in that I think we need a bit of an explanation. We're your friends, Adrik, why would you keep something like this from us?"

"I had not expected to return to Deltharduin so soon," Adrik answered honestly, looking down at the plate of now cold roast goat. "And it had been so long since I was last within these cavernous walls, it felt as though I were able to leave this life behind me, at least for a time."

"How do you just leave behind the life of ruling over an entire kingdom?" O'doc asked.

"Not an entire kingdom, O'doc," Adrik corrected with a faint smile. "The only true king of the mountains is Othar. I am but lord over one of the four thaneships that make up the Kingdom of Stone."

Enna recognized the title for the dominion of the dwarves that Varis had taught she and Erasmus all those months ago in Hallowspire. Were the dwarves aware of the true Four Kingdoms as fae-folk were? How much did they know of the true nature of arcana? How many peoples really distrusted humans with that knowledge?

"My family, Clan Thornmallet, was one of the four birthed by Uthar and Mirandira in the beginning, when their father wrought the mountains from the ground and bore our homes within them, and as such the firstborn of every generation has ruled over Morabendar as Thane." The dwarf chuckled a little. "It was never the manner of life I had wished for, yet there I was, eldest of my kin. I had a responsibility that was divinely preordained, and so for years I endured the schooling, the training, everything that was required of me until I was able to take my leave."

"Take your leave?" O'doc raised a quizzical eyebrow. "You mean to tell me a dwarven thane can just up and abandon his station?"

Adrik shook his head. "No. When I left Morabendar I was but a young man, my father still in good health, and with many years ahead of him. Evidently I lost track of time, and of his health..."

"Oh no, Adrik..." Enna began, realizing the implications. "I'm so sorry."

The dwarf let a somber smile show under his beard. "I thank you, milady, but be assured that his was a life well-lived." His smile quickly faded, a sullen furrow in his brow replacing it. "I regret, however, that I was summoned to assume my mantle amid ill tidings. I fear the centuries of peacetime among the dwarves are reaching their twilight."

"But I've heard nothing of animosities between the dwarves and the Four Kingdoms..." Professor Coldstone noted, trying to recall all his recent conversations with Caliope.

"Were that it was one of the Kingdoms..." Adrik replied grimly. "Several months ago, Goran Stouthearth, Thane of Ulbaryn was killed in a rockslide while inspecting a previously untouched area in the northwestern mountains that he had planned on utilizing for a new mining operation. Not a common dispatch, but common enough that it is rarely seen as suspicious. His brother, Zanak, ascended to the Thaneship, and as of late some of my sister's operatives from within Ulbaryn have been hearing disturbing rumours that Zanak had his brother assassinated. Some have even speculated that Zanak has some way of controlling the earth around him, and that he caused the rockslide himself. Most pressing, however, were the rumours that Zanak means to make war on Morabendar."

"Adrik!" Enna chided the dwarf. "You should have told us, you know we'd all be willing to help."

"And that, milady, is precisely why I did not tell you. This is a dwarven matter, started by dwarves, and settled by dwarves."

"If that were the case then, Adrik," Coldstone interjected, looking slightly perplexed, "then why did you tell your sister just now that we could be willing to help?"

Adrik looked over to the Professor and began to feel the warmth of embarrassment on his face. "Ah, yes. I had forgotten that you were versed in some dwarfish, Professor..." He then looked sheepishly to O'doc and Enna. "Please, do not think that I meant to speak on your behalf, nor to force you into some manner of servitude... Dwarves, especially those who scarcely venture north, are wary of any but dwarves. My sister has her apprehensions about you all, as is her prerogative as commander of my army..."

Enna stood up and walked over to where Adrik was sitting, placing her hand on his shoulder. "Adrik, you don't need to explain anything. You know that we're ready to help any way that we can, dwarves or not."

"Here here!" O'doc held a stone tumbler, still full of now lukewarm ale, into the air.

Adrik looked up at Enna, a faint, relieved smile emerging from the ornate braids of his beard. "Well then, I suppose all is settled. Perhaps we ought to adjourn for the night, I've a feeling our hot-headed companion will still require some convincing, and I am beginning to doubt that they'll be returning to finish their meals."

Erasmus half-laid in a bed that was too small for his body, gently plucking at the strings of his mandolin. The half-elf fingered a number of scales, limbering the joints in his hands after several days of having not touched the instrument, before lightly strumming a chord progression that was all at once light and morose. He closed his eyes and began to hum an old Ghestal folk song that his mother had taught him. She had never known the words, and Erasmus had never bothered to try and find them. The song was one of the few things she was able to leave him when she died. For the bard, adding lyrics would only detract from his nostalgic memories. A smile began to permeate Erasmus' lips, as it often did when he played the song, and he found himself so caught up in the melody that he did not even realize that O'doc Overhill had slipped into the room.

"I think that's the first I've seen you smile since we left Khalen Ridge," O'doc said, startling Erasmus and bringing the music to a halt.

"I suppose you'd like to chide me as well," Erasmus responded, the smile quickly fading from his face. "Sorry I didn't stick around long enough earlier for you to have a go."

"I'll not hold what happened earlier against you," O'doc said, moving a chair near the bed and hopping onto it, taking a seat on the low backrest. "It may not have been your most tactful moment, but you made some valid points. Adrik did owe us an explanation, and we got one." The halfling recounted the information that Adrik had given them at supper, as Erasmus looked at him thoughtfully. "Come morning, we're all to meet and discuss what we can do to help. No one's twisting your arm, Erasmus, but we're all hoping you'll be willing to help, too."

Erasmus laughed dryly, gazing through the halfling. "Oh, you know me, old friend. I'm nothing if not willing to help." When he noticed O'doc continuing to stare at him, he asked "Anything else?"

"Yes, as a matter of fact," O'doc replied. "There's more to this than just this business with Adrik. When we got here, you nearly tried to take Falken's head off. What is your problem with him?"

"I don't trust him." Erasmus responded flatly.

"How many people have we worked with that we didn't trust?" the halfling asked half in jest. "You always managed to be civil, until the job was done at least. And besides, I know Falken. I know he can be trusted, and I'm just as good a judge of shady characters as you."

Erasmus said nothing.

"...This is about Enna, isn't it?"

Erasmus continued to stare at the soft glow of the illuminated strips of metal along the wall, and was silent a while before he answered. "When I met Enna, when we were down in those cells below Rheth, she had no one, nothing. Everything that happened to her while we were there, being separated from her father, and everything with Varis, I tried to be there for her. I told myself I would do everything I could to help her see things through. The thing is, she's learning fast, faster than I can help. Coldstone... he can help her... I guess..." Erasmus searched a moment for the words. "I guess I feel like I failed."

O'doc got down from the chair, walked over to Erasmus, put his hand on the bard's shoulder, and met his gaze with a comforting smile. "Erasmus," he said in a soothing, sympathetic tone, "that may be the stupidest thing I have ever heard you say." He began to laugh, and Erasmus, swatting the halfling's hand away, joined the laughter in spite of himself. "I'm serious!" O'doc continued. "You're one of Enna's closest friends, if not her closest. You think she expects you to teach her how to be an arcanist? If you don't want to fail her, than get your head out of your own ass, stop sulking around, and be there for her, as a friend."

The two laughed a moment longer, and when their laughter died down, they looked at one another and smiled, as close friends do. O'doc looked thoughtfully at Erasmus. "You love her, don't you?" he asked, breaking the silence. "As a friend, I mean. A sister. You'd do anything for her, I'd gather."

"I likely would," Erasmus replied. "As any good brother would."

"I wasn't implying that you were *in* love." O'doc retorted. "I know what that looks like. I saw it that night in the tavern where we met that elven woman."

"I appreciate you leaving that little detail out when you told the others."

"Your business is your own." O'doc held his hands up defensively. "One thing, though, in all the years we've known one another, you've never told me her name."

Erasmus reclined back in his small bed and looked wistfully at the ceiling. "Zarah. Her name was Zarah."

Chapter 15

Headmaster Cresthill wrinkled his nose at the stale, sour smell of the small, dimly-lit tavern he entered. "This place smells like it's not been cleaned since the day it opened its doors."

"Oh, it's not that bad, Daylen," Lannister smiled wryly, clapping the headmaster on the arm as he strode past him into the establishment. "You're a man of station now, but I know you weren't high-born. I'm sure you spent enough of your youth in places that smelled plenty worse."

The unlikely-looking pair strode across the taproom, the halfling with the kind of arrogance of someone who was a regular at the dingy establishment, and the man with the kind of arrogance of someone who made a point of avoiding such places. "Afternoon, Ohr," Lannister nodded casually to the half-orc who kept bar. "Don't mind my friend and I, we'll just be in back." Ohr nodded absently, the look on his face giving Cresthill the impression that their presence, or perhaps just the halfling's presence, was a common enough occurrence to be an annoyance, though uncommon enough that the barkeep was able to tolerate it.

The two came to a plain-looking wooden door at the far side of the taproom, which led to a long, dark stone hallway. Looking upward at the arcanist, Lannister motioned for him to enter. "After you, Headmaster."

The halfling had brought Cresthill out to Frostpoint in the middle of the night, telling him nothing past that there was a contact whom he ought to meet. When they arrived in the small town, the dim, filthy, all-but-abandoned tavern in which they stood was their immediate destination. Neither of these facts gave the headmaster much pause. As Lannister had said, he was not high-born, and shady situations in disreputable locales were not uncommon, even in Lohvast. This strange, unremarkable doorway, and the pitch-black corridor past it, however, filled Cresthill with unease, though he fought not to show it.

"Come now, Daylen," Lannister smiled, sensing Cresthill's hesitation. "You're not afraid of the dark, I'm sure." When the headmaster remained still and stone-faced, the halfling rolled his eyes. "Oh, very well, but be a dear and make some light, and make sure to shut the door behind you."

The headmaster nodded stoically, whispering the words in Elvish to cause a bright white light to emanate from the amulet around his neck. As he closed the wooden door behind him and looked forward, he saw that the corridor stretched long, impossibly so. The headmaster walked behind Lannister, trying to fathom what was going on around him.

"Queer bit of architecture, isn't it?" Lannister commented, addressing feelings that the headmaster had not voiced. "I didn't understand how it worked either, the first time. All told, I still don't quite get it." The two said little else as they descended a spiral stone staircase, reaching a wooden door at the bottom emblazoned with a symbol the headmaster did not recognize, some kind of sigil or brand. "I've seen the inside of your office, Daylen," the halfling said as he began to open the door and step through, "and it seems only polite that I should invite you into mine."

Daylen Cresthill stepped through the threshold, dispelling his light as he did, into a huge chamber that was as impossibly tall as the corridor had been long. The first thing to catch the headmaster's eye was the tall bookshelves that stood row-on-row on either side of the large middle aisle, though what really caught his attention was the immense energy that he felt surging through it. He said nothing, simply standing in awe.

"I've always thought this place a bit drab, myself," Lannister broke Cresthill's silent, wondering haze, and climbed up to sit on a nearby tabletop. "Might be the fact that I'm not the most learned person. Never saw much use for books, unless they were ledgers." The halfling looked around almost absentmindedly as he spoke. "Old tales about gods, kings, and heroes are a fine way of putting a babe to sleep, but come the end of the day, you're better off using that parchment to keep track of what you got, and what you haven't."

"Can you not read?" Cresthill looked over at the halfling.

"I taught myself what I needed to survive, progress." Lannister hopped off the tabletop, sauntering over to a nearby shelf. "You don't get to a position like mine by being completely illiterate." He pulled an old tome from the shelf and began to quickly leaf through the pages. "But these books... I may not be the best reader, but I know the shapes of all the common letters. The letters in these books down here, though, they're something else altogether."

Cresthill moved to speak, but was interrupted by a light, high-pitched meow. Leaping up onto the table on which Lannister had been sitting was a sleek gray cat. "Oh, hello!" the headmaster said, gently running his hand along its slender back as it purred contentedly. "What's your name? You're the barkeep's mouser, no doubt."

Lannister, hearing the purring, turned around and walked back toward the table. "Her name's Zarah, and I can assure you she makes a point of not killing rodents unless I give her order to. She's our contact." The cat proceeded to crawl up into the headmaster's lap and continue purring, causing Cresthill to look at the halfling with complete incredulity. Lannister looked sternly at the cat.

"Alright, Zarah, you've had your fun, but I don't pay you to sit in men's laps and purr for them."

The cat looked up at the halfling with large yellow eyes, before hopping down from the headmaster's lap indifferently, beginning what looked to Cresthill to stretch out as a cat does. Slowly, however, the stretch persisted, and the cat elongated and grew, the gray coat, tail, and whiskers all dissipating, and the slender feline body replaced itself with the tall slender body of an elven woman with silvery black hair, with eyes that were of a similarly jaundiced tone to Lannister's. She stood there, naked, and smirked playfully at the headmaster, who immediately averted his eyes out of a combination of respect and embarrassment.

"You couldn't have just shown up already changed?" Lannister looked at the elf irritably "Or clothed, for that matter?"

"You know as well as I do that I couldn't very well just leave a wardrobe lying about." She responded matter-of-factly. "And I've had scarce little time in my natural form lately." She looked back at Cresthill. "Although I dare say, perching up on your lap felt plenty natural to me."

Lannister shook his head and turned to the headmaster. "Daylen, may I present Zarah, one of my best agents. Zarah, this is Daylen Cresthill, Headmaster of the Arcane University."

The headmaster, feeling himself begin to come to terms with what had just taken place, turned his back to the elf, and began to take off the heavy robes he had worn for the trip. "Here, my dear," he held the robes outstretched behind him, "be my guest."

"Quite the gentleman," Zarah replied, taking the robes and wrapping them around herself. "I almost hate to ask what you're doing associating with someone like Lannister Ravenclaw." The headmaster had turned back around, and was now looking at the elf with a studious gaze. "You know," she said, taking note of Cresthill's expression, "if you hadn't been such a gentleman, I'd feel a bit slighted that you weren't staring like that when I was naked."

"Apologies, my dear," Cresthill's gaze was unchanging. "I had heard of werewolves, wererats, even wereboars, but never a cat..."

"Probably because we know better than to tread about openly in Lohvast," Zarah retorted. "I can think of a few reasons why people ought to lock me up, but lycanthropy isn't one of them."

"What is that supposed to mean?" Cresthill asked, a bit taken aback. "Those inflicted with lycanthropy are treated with care and compassion in Lohvast, not like Hallowspire where they cull those who suffer."

Zarah let out a short, derisive laugh. "Do you hear yourself, friend? Speaking about my gift as though I were no better than a leper. We lycanthropes can live as both beast and biped, taking whatever form suits us at any given moment."

"But the madness, and the illness..."

"Are rare, especially among fae." The elf maintained her smirk, but waved her hand dismissively. "And the price is far outweighed by the payoff."

Lannister cleared his throat to direct attention to himself. "Speaking of payoff, I'm not paying you to sit about here and chat."

Zarah glared momentarily at the halfling before looking back to Cresthill. "I do so hate it when the boss is right. Follow me." She led the two back toward the wooden door from which they had entered, and back up the spiral staircase. As they reached the top of the staircase, however, they were met not with the long corridor down which Cresthill and Lannister had come, but instead the group emerged in a large manorial room, a few candles flickering in the dark, and the pale moonlight pouring in from a large window. The room appeared to be some manner of study, with a desk, several bookshelves, and small couch, all of which were littered with books and scrolls.

"I don't understand..." the headmaster stammered. "How did... where...?"

"I'll admit I'm a bit surprised myself that this worked." Lannister looked about the room. "I really just based that on a hunch."

"Welcome to East Fellowdale, gentlemen." Zarah bowed. "Specifically to the home of Professor Falken Coldstone. The Professor has taken leave on a personal issue, so I'll be your hostess. Make yourselves at home."

Chapter 16

I t took nearly two weeks, and very gradual diplomacy on the part of Adrik, but eventually, Merida had conceded to take the help that had been offered to her by her brother's companions. In that time, at the dwarf's behest, the four dedicated themselves to sharpening their abilities. In Enna's case, this meant spending the majority of her time awake with the Professor. Unlike in the Four Kingdoms, the dwarves had no practiced arcanists, so to speak, and so while Erasmus and O'doc were more than willing to hone their martial prowess with members of Morabendar's army, more often than not Enna spent her days studying under the Professor, learning whatever he was willing to teach, though oftentimes having to keep him on track with their lessons.

"So clever, these devices. Runelamps, the dwarves call them. I've found they even dim in relative accordance with the sun! It really is quite fascinating, my dear, isn't it?" he thought aloud one day as the two worked in a large stretch of caves that served as the stables for the gryphons that the Morabendine cavalry used, and was housing the

Overhill's owls. "No outright use of arcana, and yet inventions like this." The Professor ran his hand along one of the luminescent strips that were seemingly everywhere in Deltharduin. "Do you know what these are, Enna?"

The elf shook her head, and moved to say something to guide Coldstone's wandering mind back to the matters at hand, but was an instant too slow.

"Nor did I when we first arrived, and it plagued me so!" This was not an exaggeration, Enna noted, as not a day passed during their time in the Dwarven city in which the man did not spend some time pondering on the subject. "Then it dawned on me: these runes! They don't look traditionally Elven, though they are! Elven runes carved by Dwarven hands, losing the beautiful flow one expects, and taking on the kind of rigidity one sees in traditional Dwarven runes. I asked several people in Deltharduin, and there are examples throughout these thaneships!" He took Enna's hand and led her excitedly to one of the nests in which a gryphon rested. "The gryphons all wear anklets," he explained, pointing at one of the resting creatures' large outstretched paws. "They correspond to staves wielded by their riders. I examined one such staff, and do you know what I found? The words of a charm spell! The methods are different, but the power, the outcome, it's no different from what you and I are able to do!"

"Speaking of which, Professor," Enna interjected, finally seeing an opening, "I think I'm starting to better my own abilities."

"Oh?" Enna could practically see the man's mind switching focus. "Please, my dear, do tell."

She led the Professor back from the stables, out into the large cavern. She picked up a stone from the ground, roughly half the size of her fist, and tossed it to him, proceeding to step back roughly eight feet. "Alright, Professor," she looked back at him with a hopeful glint in her eye, "I want you to try and throw the stone at me."

"...I'm sorry?"

"That stone, I want you to try and hit me with it." The elf made it sound as if her request were the most natural thing in the world. "Trust me," she said, drawing forth her club and standing at the ready.

"If you insist..." the Professor replied hesitantly. He wound back the arm holding the stone, unwound, and released.

Enna watched the small projectile hurl toward her, and holding out her club, her implement, called out the wind evocation spell she had uttered what seemed like a lifetime ago in Rheth, and had been one of her most practiced spells in the months since.

"A AMIN 'I SUL!"

Enna felt the familiar rush of arcane energy tingle through her body and out the head of the club, and watched as the elemental force she conjured rushed outward from her. Contrary to what she had hoped, however, the wind did not stop the stone, nor even slow it down. Rather the small projectile whizzed through the wind, thankfully coming up short of her and landing with a tumble a foot or so in front of her.

"You didn't throw it hard enough," Enna protested, her voice evidently deflated by the outcome of her little experiment.

"And if I had?" Coldstone asked closing the gap between them. "My dear, I don't much feel like explaining to the others how, after I whisked you away from the city proper for an afternoon, you ended up with a blackened eye."

Enna frowned, bending over to pick up the stone and examine it. "I don't understand... Professor, I told you about that day in Rheth..."

"You have, and I believe every word of the story."

"So why can't I do that now? Why was I only ever able to cast a spell that powerful then?"

"Enna, I wish that I had a clear answer for you," Coldstone shook his head. "People can be capable of fantastic feats when in moments of distress, and I have no doubt that played a part. Past that, however..." the Professor shrugged, unsure of what to tell her. "No matter, however. One has no business trying to use the wind to protect themselves from anything besides an especially malevolent kite. I think I ought to teach you a spell of shielding." He stepped back to his original position, and drew out his wand. "Now, my dear," he said, grinning at Enna, "I want you to throw that stone at me this time. Don't fret, the others will think less of an errant bruise on me than they will on you."

Enna smirked back at the Professor, and winding up, released the stone with all her might. Coldstone readied himself to cast his spell, but almost immediately after the stone left Enna's hand, it stopped and hung in midair, as still as though it were still on the ground. The two arcanists approached the stone slowly, cautiously, until both were mere inches from it. They shared a look, confirming with one another that the trick was neither of their doing, and as the Professor began to raise his hand toward the stone, it darted away, quickly traveling further into the cavern, so fast and so far that neither he nor Enna were able to spot where it went exactly.

"...Hello?" Enna cried out in the direction the stone had flown. "...Is anybody there?"

There was no response, but after a long pause, the pair heard a low rumbling coming from the darkness. The two stood in silence as rumbling persisted for some time, before gradually petering out. Coldstone moved to speak, but immediately stopped himself when a second sound could be heard in the darkness, a heavy, rhythmic sound, like that of giant footsteps that were quickly nearing.

"Quick, to the stable!" Enna whispered hoarsely, taking the Professor by the hand and nearly dragging him over to the structure to hide. The two crouched low inside the small stone building, listening intently as the thunderous steps grew nearer, though neither moved so much as to even hazard a glance through a door frame at the source of the sound. As the footfalls reached their loudest, nearest point, the sound of the gryphons and owls startling and panicking only barely audible over the clamour of movement outside, Enna clung to the Professor's arm, afraid, until she realized that the steps quieted and distanced themselves as quickly as they had approached. When the steps no longer echoed through the cavern, both Enna and Coldstone let out a sigh of relief. The Professor stood, helping Enna to her feet, and both, as if to try and mend their frayed nerves, went to work calming the animals.

Neither said anything for a long while as the shushed and caressed the large beasts and birds. Enna's thoughts were filled with questions, however. What had happened? Had she and Falken mistakenly done something to cause it? What entered that cavern, and why had it bypassed them completely? Where was it headed, if anywhere? The last question stuck in the elf's mind, and a look of horror spread across her face as she began to recount what Adrik had told them when they arrived in Morabendar, about the thane of Ulbaren, Zanak, some said that he could control the earth around him, Adrik had told them.

The stone had floated in front of them, then flown away in the direction the noise came from.

"Falken," Enna clutched Coldstone's arm, her face pale with fear, and her eyes filled with panic, "we need to get back to the city, now."

By the time Enna and Falken reached the outermost edge Deltharduin proper, they had already begun to see signs of destruction that was wrought by whatever had passed them back at the stables. The roads leading further into the city were littered with craters that were large and shallow. Alarm bells could be heard echoing all about the city, and the dwarves who did not scatter into their homes for security were wandering the streets panic-stricken and distraught. Past the craters, little if any damage was done to most of the city. The monstrous footsteps seemed to move in a single path, never straying from the main roads that led to the centre of Deltharduin, to Citadel Moraben. Even if there had been no footprints to follow, the creature's goal was apparently met in light of the fact that the citadel, normally seen from anywhere in the city, was no longer visible. Instead, an eerie halo of dust and debris that had not yet settled lingered in the wake of the citadel's doubtless collapse.

Enna and Falken arrived at the fallen structure, trying to make sense of the situation that transpired amid the scrambling scores of Morabendine soldiers and unarmed citizens alike. When all Enna saw was dwarves, however, a knot began to form in the pit of her stomach. Where were Erasmus and O'doc? They were supposed to have been training with Merida in the citadel's barracks today, and they should have been nearby.

As if in answer to the questions in her mind, Enna heard a voice from behind her. "Summerlark! Coldstone!" The elf and the Professor spun on their heels to see Merida Mettlehelm. The dwarf looked filthy and unkempt, dust and grime mixing with the sweat on her brow, several strands of hair that escaped her ornate braids stuck to the filthy paste.

"Lady Merida!" Falken called out as he and Enna quickly walked toward her. "By the gods, what happened?"

"Was running drills with the troops when the bells rang," she explained, wiping her dirty brow with her equally dirty gauntlet. "Thought it was just the midday ringing at first, then they didn't stop. Young page came down to the barracks, told me we were under attack by some rock monster, and the thane ordered all the buildings evacuated." Her breathing was laboured as she spoke, though she declined when Enna offered a drink from her small water skin. "Wouldn't have believed it had I not seen it with my own eyes... a creature... two legs, two arms... made all of stone, nearly thirty feet tall, I'd say. Walked up to the citadel, it had been near totally evacuated, save for those of us who took up defense of it, your friends included." There was a distance in the dwarf's eyes, as if she were recollecting what had happened, trying to put words to it. "It... started to float, the rock creature, and it changed, just turned into a floating pile of stone. Artillery fired crossbow bolts, those were useless. The thing floated up, until it was overtop the citadel, and it came apart. It was like a whole thirty foot stretch of mineshaft all collapsed on top of the citadel."

"Where are Erasmus and O'doc?" Enna asked, who had been looking nervously about as Merida had explained what happened.

When Enna looked back at the dwarf, her expression was still that of a stern-faced commander, but her eyes belied the fact that she was hesitant to answer. "The both of them were aiding in the evacuation..." she paused, swallowing hard and averting Enna's gaze. "If that damned half-elf had just listened to my orders..."

The knot in Enna's stomach worsened, making her feel as if she were about to be sick. She covered her mouth with her hands, fearing the worst, and fighting back the tears that accompanied that fear. "Merida..." she said, just barely above a whisper, fearing anything more would cause her to break down.

"...There were falling rocks..." Merida answered finally. "Stonehand saw them, broke position, dove to shove me out of the way of them. Damned fairy-bastard got pinned underneath them."

Enna couldn't speak, for if she so much as opened her mouth, all that would come out would be heavy sobs. She clutched Falken's arm, burying her face in his sleeve and fighting not to dissolve into a blubbering mess. The Professor looked at Merida. "Is he..."

"Not yet..." the dwarf shook her head slowly. "Overhill and some of the others carted him off, and, Othar willing, my husband will make sure he doesn't."

This answer offered Enna some relief. Adrik had spoken some of his brother-in-law Morgran, the former court cleric to the thane of Harbak, and had not once spoke ill of him or his medical abilities. The elf raised her face from Falken's robed arm, her eyes red under the strain of fighting back tears. "My apologies, milady, I..."

Merida waved away the apology. "You're young, Summerlark, inexperienced with this sort of thing." She turned and began to walk, beckoning the two to follow. "Come, I'll take you to the temple of Othar, we'll see if Morgran can't call down a miracle."

Chapter 17

Lannister Ravenclaw smiled contentedly to himself, quietly sipping at a flagon of ale as he sat in the taproom of the Merchant's Quilt. Since coming into Queen Merrian's employ, he had little time to simply kick up his feet and relax due to his dual responsibilities of being Lohvast's royal spy and maintaining his control over the River Rats. The latter would have been more difficult, to be sure, were it not for the fact that the recent powers granted to the halfling were able to quickly silence any potential dissenters within the guild's ranks.

He had earned himself a break, he reasoned, given the position he was in. Cresthill was a perfect tool, devouring the plethora of information at his disposal in that manor, still so enthralled by the Queen's charming vex that he never once questioned the legitimacy of what he was doing, doubly so thanks to Zarah playing the perfect little hostess. The elf could drive Lannister perfectly mad with her insatiable cockiness, but she had been a greater asset in recent months than he could ever have asked for. After all, she had not only been instrumental in finding Coldstone's manor, but in doing so she had

inadvertently offered Lannister a link to O'doc
Overhill. Lannister's smile wavered, as for months
now he was forced to put the halfling and his cohorts
in the back of his mind while he tended to the Rats
and served the Mission. Now, however, he had his
key to revenge, and it came in the form of a robed
halfling woman, her hair littered with streaks of gray,
who sat alone at a table near the taproom's hearth,
every so often glancing expectantly at the tavern
entrance.

Lannister recalled the information Zarah had
given him. The elf had seen the halfling with
Coldstone on occasion, the two usually meeting in
this tavern. He hadn't paid much heed to the elf's
reports until some weeks back, when word had
reached him that this halfling had brought some
acquaintances to the Professor's manor whose
descriptions matched those of Overhill and his
cohorts. O'doc had always managed to keep his work
at arm's length from his personal life, Lannister
mused, even when the two had been partners.
Lannister had always respected that about O'doc,
even though it had made it nearly impossible to gain
any kind of leverage on the little sneak. This time,
however, he finally slipped up. Overhill knew this
halfling somehow, and Lannister was prepared to use
any means possible to extract that information.

The halfling woman looked around the
taproom once more, her expression shifting subtly
from expectation to worry before collecting herself
from the table and exiting the tavern. Lannister

waited before tossing a few coins on the table and exiting himself. The halfling had spent plenty of time tailing people through city streets, enough to know that the woman would be easy to stalk, but more than enough to know that he ought to use caution nonetheless. The sun began to hang low in the sky, casting shadows all around the city, and the streets were just busy enough that a halfling could be easily spotted, provided they weren't actively avoiding being seen. Lannister moved easily among the crowds, only needing to find cover the few times his quarry had made an unexpected turn down a street, and only stopping once she had reached her initial destination, the temple of Shendre.

Lannister cursed under his breath as he waited at the opposite side of the road. He had forgotten that Zarah had mentioned that this halfling was a priestess. He didn't like temples and priests; they were a lot of superstitious nonsense and judgmental bookworms. Lannister made a point of avoiding hallowed ground because, as a thief, temples were the worst targets. True, some of the followers believed that their gods favoured offerings of coin or jewels, but the few times he had ever attempted to case a temple in his adult life, no matter the temple and no matter the disguise, Lannister always felt like he stuck out, like those damned priests could spot him from a mile away, similar to how he'd felt in Delverbrook the day he was branded with all eyes fixed on him. The memory made the scar on his shoulder ache and caused him to uncontrollably shudder, so much so that he nearly missed the opportunity when his quarry, the priestess, exited the temple and continued down the road.

Lannister continued the hunt in his practiced way, following every step the priestess took until she arrived at Professor Coldstone's manor. Ever since he had begun to contemplate following this woman, knowing that she was his connection back to Overhill, he had been thinking of how best to use her to hurt his former partner. Killing her would likely have been the simplest option, but by that token it would also be the least satisfying. Seduction was unreliable, at best, and hardly the pallid-looking Ravenclaw's forte. He had considered making her an agent of the Mission, but that was a drawn-out process that he doubted he had the time for, doubly so upon learning that she was a damned priestess.

The sun had almost completely been enveloped by the horizon now, blanketing most of the city in an inky, overcast sky, making it all the easier for Lannister as he crept up behind the woman. He grinned his crooked, yellow smile, satisfied that he knew exactly how to get Overhill right where he wanted him. The thought of the plan had Lannister so elated, in fact, that he was not even bothered by the discomfort of holding his transformation at the halfway point.

Caliope Hollowpot was worried. Falken Coldstone was absentminded, at best, and downright inept at worst, but never, in all the years that she had known the man, had he ever missed their lunches. She had assumed that maybe he was with O'doc and his friends, but she had not heard from them either. As much as it was entirely possible that the whole thing was nothing, it felt very much like something. She had stopped by the temple on the way over to the manor and said a quick prayer, just to be sure. She could see light from the windows. It probably was nothing, she reasoned. They were all of them likely caught up in the excitement of this whole thing. She would walk up to Falken's door and knock on it, and when he answered she would chide him for forgetting their lunch. Caliope began to smirk and shook her head. O'doc would be hearing an earful, too, she reasoned, worrying his aunt so. The halfling was not five feet from the manor's front door, however, when she felt a furry hand with long fingers wrap around her mouth, muffling her cry of pain as she felt what could only be long, jagged teeth clamping down into her shoulder. She wanted to resist, to turn and face her attacker, but a thick, sickly feeling washed quickly over her, making her arms and legs feel leaden and her head light. Her vision blurred a moment, and she felt as though she was going to be sick, but before she could, the weight added to her extremities moved upward into her head and face, causing her head to loll about uselessly in front of her before she slipped into the blackness of unconsciousness.

ChapTer 18

The temple of Othar in Deltharduin sat at the city's southern most point; an intricate, angular building carved into the rock wall that had existed in the cavern some centuries ago, before the southward expansion of Morabendar. The temple itself was all that substantially remained of the rock face, making it a huge squared tower that began at road level and ended ten stories above at the ceiling of the dwarven city, as much a structural pillar as a moral one.

Falken and Enna followed the sprinting Merida Mettlehelm as she guided them away from the ruined Citadel Moraben towards the temple. Enna was told that Erasmus was being tended to there at the head cleric's chambers located on the ground floor. The three hurried into the temple's main hall, a large octagonal room with rows of stonework benches surrounding a marble dais in the centre. Branching out from the dais were pathways branching out in four directions, one being the entrance, and three ending in large marble effigies of Othar, lord of all dwarves, and his children Uthar and Mirandira. At the foot of the statue of Othar, kneeling in robes whose finery was marred, torn, and dirty due to recent events, was Adrik Thornmallet.

"Adrik!" Enna cried out, running past Merida and Falken toward the dwarf, her voice bouncing off a hundred different surfaces inside the temple, "What's happening? Are you alright? Where are Erasmus and O'doc?"

Adrik raised a hand to stay Enna's barrage of questions, and looked up at her with a face that bore a look of solemnity and exhaustion in equal measure. "Ah, milady, it warms my heart to see the only two arcanists in Morabendar are unharmed amid this chaos," he smiled wearily. "I am fine. I was dragged from Citadel Moraben by overeager stewards at first sound of the alarm bells, much to my consternation."

"They were doing as I bade," Merida interjected. "Ensuring the safety of the Thane."

"If I must sit idly in some safe house when Deltharduin is in danger than I am not befit for the title," he retorted. "What use is the safety of the Thane over the safety of his thaneship?"

"Lord and scions, Adrik, this impulsiveness of yours may have suited your decision to run from your responsibilities, but you're not the coal-bearded youth you once were. This was an act of war, and whether you care for it or not, in a war the thane needs protection."

"I am perfectly capable of protecting myself, Merida. Othar's beard, I kept myself alive for the last thirty years without having stubble-chinned whelps at my beck and call!"

"Kept yourself alive against what, tell?" Merida snapped back. "Ill-trained brigands? The occasional filthy goblin-kin? Tell me brother, how often while you were off playing wayward merchant in the north did you need to defend yourself from actual professional soldiers, or damned giant stone creatures? You worry about your safety, brother, and leave the defense of the thaneship to those of us who've spent our lives defending it."

Falken cleared his throat audibly before Adrik could continue to prod at what was evidently an old wound. "Let's just all be glad that those of us present are all in good health, and perhaps address the matter of those who may not be?"

Adrik deflated some, running his hand down his beard. "Of course, Professor. This whole calamitous ordeal has wrought my nerves thoroughly. Forgive my ill-temper. I trust you are aware of what happened?"

"I explained," Merida nodded.

Adrik returned the nod slowly. "Master O'doc is unharmed, Othar be thanked, though he has refused to leave Master Erasmus."

"Where are they now?" Enna asked.

"In Brother Morgran's ritual room." Adrik motioned to a door to the right of the statue in front of them.

"Can we..." Enna began tentatively, "Would we be interrupting if we..."

"Go on," Merida nodded at the door. "It'd take more than a handful of peeping northerners to break my husband's concentration, especially when there's a life at stake."

"You aren't coming?" Falken asked the dwarves.

Merida shook her head. "Deltharduin just received everything short of a formal declaration of war. As commander of the Morabendine army, I must consult my Thane, whether it suits him or not."

Adrik looked up at the arcanists, the tired smile returned to his face "We will enter as soon as is possible," he said reassuringly.

Falken and Enna walked through the door into a relatively small room. The room was uncommonly dark, as it had been one of the first times since the group had arrived in the mountains that there were no runelamps emanating their soft white glow. Rather, the dim light from four stone wall sconces cast odd shadows throughout the room. In the centre of the room was a large slab-like table upon which lay Erasmus Stonehand, bruised and bloodied, his legs twisted ways in which they were not meant to. The half-elf's eyes were closed, but his chest moved with steady, if shallow breaths. Standing over the unconscious half-elf was a dwarf in robes of deep blue and gold. His long hair and beard were a burnt orange that hinged on brown, and though he kept none of it braided or tied, there was nothing unkempt about it. The dwarf's face was one of pure concentration and he laid what appeared to be a number of tiles along the table's edge, all the while softly murmuring something Enna could only have assumed was Dwarfish. To one side of the room's far end sat a small desk and a number of shelves containing books, scrolls, mysterious jars, and more of the strange tiles. The desk chair, little more than a padded metalwork stool, was currently being occupied by O'doc Overhill, who looked on nervously, as though it took all of his resolve not to leap up from where he sat. The halfling was so fixated on his wounded friend, he nearly swooned as Enna and Falken approached him.

"When did you get here?" he whispered hoarsely.

"Only a moment ago," Enna replied. She gave a quick sidelong glance toward the centre of the room, her eyes unable to linger on her friend's twisted and broken form. "How is he?"

O'doc shook his head slowly, as unable to turn from the scene as Enna was to face it. "I've seen Erasmus get tossed about, take his fair share of blows, but nothing like this." The halfling's eyes were distant. "You wouldn't know to look at him right now, but he's in pain. Brother Morgran had to give him some kind of herb to calm him down. It put him right out, and I think that's for the best."

"A herb?" Falken noted. "Some manner of a root, was it? Boiled in a tea or swallowed, or..."

"Falken," Enna's voice had a slight edge to it. "Now isn't really the time."

The Professor frowned at himself. "Of course, my apologies." He turned back to face O'doc. "Has Brother Morgran spoken at all of what he's doing?"

"Barely a word past his mutterings in Dwarfish. When we arrived he told me and the others who brought Erasmus here to lay him on that table, and when I didn't leave he just sort of looked at me a moment, told me to sit here and wait, and then went about his ritual."

"A ritual that is now nearly complete," Brother Morgran spoke, turning around to face them. He had a deep, low voice similar to Adrik's, but with a thick accent indicative of a dwarf who rarely spoke in anything other than his native tongue. "The runes are set, and the prayers have been made."

"So what now, Brother?" O'doc asked.

"We await Othar's blessing," the dwarf replied simply. He looked over the halfling, the elf, and the human. "I should warn you, when the ritual begins, it will be painful for him, more so even than the salve I applied can block. I will not think ill of you for excusing yourselves now."

The companions looked to one another, then back to Brother Morgran. Enna shook her head resolutely. "We will stay, if it's all the same."

The cleric, whose expressions had up to this point been unreadable, let a wry smile appear on his face. "By the Lord and his scions, you northerners are made of tougher stuff than my wife credits you."

Before anyone could respond, they all turned to the table, as a low humming began to emanate from the tiles surrounding it. A soft glow rose from the tiles, illuminating the unconscious half-elf within it, but bright enough to obscure anyone's view. Once

Erasmus was fully enveloped by the light, he began to writhe about on the table, his body moving in such a way that it was obvious he was not in control of it. It was then that the group could hear the audible popping of several bones being thrust back into place. It was only the first few pops that were heard, however, as any noise made subsequently was drowned out by the sound of Erasmus springing back into consciousness with a painful, ear-splitting cry of pain, followed by another, and another. Every bone mended, every bruise faded, and every cut sealed caused another scream to burst from the half-elf. After what seemed like an eternity to those witnessing it, the glow subsided, the cries ceased, and Erasmus went slack atop the table.

After a moment, Brother Morgran approached the half-elf, who appeared to have fallen back unconscious. The dwarf laid his hands on Erasmus' chest a moment, nodding. "Shock didn't kill him, that's good," he noted, half to himself, before turning around to face the others. "Didn't know how that would have turned out. Never performed a blessing on human nor fae, never mind half of each. Seems Othar smiles on your friend." He turned back to the table and began collecting the tiles. "He'll be needing rest. Best you leave him be some time. Stay if you like, but let him rouse himself before you think of taking him from here."

The three exited the ritual room together, sitting on the nearest bench they could find. Adrik and Merida had left, no doubt to discuss what to do next, leaving Enna, O'doc, and even Falken, who under different circumstances would have loved nothing more than to have asked Brother Morgran a hundred questions about what had just happened, to sit in silence, waiting on bated breath for Erasmus to rouse.

Chapter 19

Nebalsus sat atop the grotesque throne that served as the ironic focal point of its prison. The demon's eyes were closed as it sat deep in meditation, focusing on each of its followers, one after the other, passing quickly through the scores of unremarkable servants, and occasionally pausing for a moment to contemplate the odd member of the mortal dregs that showed a modicum of potential. Existence for Nebalsus had been painful and slow-going since the great change of power in the infernal realm some centuries ago, before the demon's fall.

Now, Nebalsus was weak, relegated to the cell in which it currently resided, tumbling endlessly through a void from which it could not reach the infernal realm to reassert power. The fact that the demon had no sway over its kin had, with time, begun to matter little to it, however. This was not for the sake of guilt, which was an emotion that effectively did not exist within the terrible ageless beings, nor was it for lack of desire, which would be equally inconceivable among the infernal. Rather, in the time it spent in near total solitude, Nebalsus had gained a dangerous edge over those who trapped it, for the demon had developed patience.

The oversight by Nebalsus' jailers was slight, at best. A single, nearly unnoticeable gap in the spell woven to keep the demon from reaching out to other realms. The weak point was not so substantial that Nebalsus could contact the mortal realm directly, but the demon had learned better than to forgo long-term success for the sake of pride. Much as it longed to see the pure fear in the eyes of mortals who looked upon it, Nebalsus was acutely aware of the satisfaction it would gain seeing the fear in the eyes of those who enslaved it when it invaded and reclaimed its place.

For the time being, Nebalsus reveled in what it was capable of. Its ability to hold numerous mortals in its thrall proved as enjoyable as it was useful, serving as a perfect means by which to amass an army. With the Nebalsus' direction, these mortals would be able to locate the seals to its prison, and would be all too willing to follow the demon into the very depths of the infernal realm.

The plan was not flawless, of course. The mortal beings were often fickle and egotistical beyond their means. The perfect example lay in the dwarf onto whom Nebalsus was currently affixed. Granted, in some aspects, the demon was grateful for this Zanak. The dwarves were always a superstitious people, so the fact that this one had tampered with one of the prison seals after stumbling upon it was nothing short of dumb luck, but that he was the younger brother of a nominal leader was as much a benefit as a point of contention. On the one hand, Zanak's notable jealousy of his brother made him an easy target, wishing for little more than his brother's place among his people as recompense for his allegiance. On the other, the dwarf seemed to get sidetracked with his own lust for menial local power. This was the problem inherent in so many of Nebalsus' more prominent acolytes, and the demon only hoped that the dwarf proved as cunning as Merrian of Lohvast, whose actions were at least in line with the Mission. The demon had waited long for its freedom, and with so many players beginning to fall into place, it wished to have to discard as few of them as possible.

Thane Zanak knelt in the small stone room tucked deep within the recesses of a cave south of Ulbaryn's capital, waiting for the obelisks to alight that he might speak with Him. While trying his best to remain stoic and solemn, the dwarf could not help but allow the slightest smile through his thick brown beard. He was pleased, not only by his own abilities, but also in how he showcased them, and he was confident that he was serving the Mission well. Some moments passed before the bright light of the obelisks began to pour onto the central dais, revealing the glowing visage of the robed figure without whom Zanak would still be in the shadow of his brother.

"You come to this summons bearing good news, Thane Zanak?" the simulacrum spoke in its impossible monotone.

"Aye, I have." Zanak bowed low, the disquieting sound of the voice making it much easier to contain his glee. "As we speak, a golem of stone, pulled right from Othar's belly, and a construct that I was able to will into existence, is no doubt sending a powerful, deadly message to the people of Deltharduin."

The spectral, robed figure was silent long enough to erase any trace of a smile from the Thane completely. "Thane Zanak," the voice spoke finally, "you were granted a gift, the only stipulation of which being that you use it in service of the Mission..." The dwarf's palms began to feel clammy, and his mind began to race. "In what way has your trick succeeded in this?"

"I..." Zanak stammered, beginning to feel a heat beneath his robes, and knowing its source all too well. "How am I to serve the Mission with the worry that the other thaneships may attack me in kind? Surely you understand..."

The dwarf was cut short by the sharp burning of the brand on his back, so sudden and potent that it forced the air from his lungs and caused him to crumple to the ground on all fours. "Do not think us a fool, Thane Zanak," the simulacrum chided as cooly and even-toned as it had begun the conversation. "We are aware that the dwarven thaneships have coexisted peacefully for centuries, and that the Otharine people are of little interest to the Mission. We do not have patience for one who wishes to use his gifts for his own megalomania."

"Wait!" Zanak cried out between gulps of air. "There are more than just dwarves in Morabendar! Thane Adrik... has brought northerners... arcanists and fae-folk...please!"

Without words or movement, the burning of the brand ceased as suddenly as it had exploded, and Zanak collapsed onto his stomach, panting and wheezing.

"Bring the... fae folk... here," the simulacrum spoke. "If they indeed exist, failure will not be tolerated."

With the suddenness of a candle being doused with water, the simulacrum vanished, and the light from the obelisks extinguished, leaving Thane Zanak in a heap on the cold, pitch-dark floor. His only thought was on mounting a full assault on Morabendar.

Chapter 20

E nna woke to a small hand nudging her. Her neck and back were stiff, and when the fuzziness of sleep cleared from her mind, she realized that she had fallen asleep on one of the cool, hard pews inside the temple of Othar, and that the hand that roused her belonged to O'doc Overhill.

"When did I fall asleep?" the elf asked, sitting up and trying to stretch the stiffness from her neck.

"Hard to say." O'doc shrugged. "The midnight bells only just rang. Seems we all dozed off, though," he motioned next to Enna, where Falken Coldstone lay still sleeping. He let out a short snore, and Enna shook her head and smiled wearily.

"Has Erasmus..." she began to ask, but O'doc simply shook his head.

"Not that I can tell," the halfling replied. "I checked on him when I woke. It doesn't look like he's moved."

"You'll have to excuse me then, O'doc," Enna looked at the halfling, her weariness giving birth to the mild annoyance one gets from an interrupted rest, "but why did you just wake me?"

"It was one of the priests that woke me, and we need to wake Falken, too." O'doc said plainly. "Adrik and his sister need to see us."

The pair roused the Professor, and together the three ascended several floors to a small, discreet meeting room in the temple's east wing. On their way they passed Brother Morgran, who himself seemed to be leaving the meeting room.

"Off to retire for the night, Brother?" Falken asked the dwarf as they crossed paths.

Morgran shook his head. "There's much to be done now, and I've no doubt Merida will be some time yet. Meantime I'll keep an eye on the half-elf, an' busy myself with other matters."

"Are you not the least bit tired?" Enna looked at the cleric sympathetically.

Morgran smiled knowingly at the elf. "Fae-child, I've been a husband nearly as long as I've been a servant of Othar, and I've learned a great many thing in my years, not least of which is that while it's near impossible to never go to sleep angry, the very least you can do is to never go to sleep apart." The dwarf nodded to the three and headed past them, adding belatedly, "I'll come for you if the half-elf wakes."

The dwarf's words had made Enna smile, and reminded her of her own parents. She realized then that she had not sent word to them since arriving in East Fellowdale. She would have to ask Adrik if there were some way for word to reach them from Morabendar, she resolved. The three walked through the doorway to see Adrik and Merida hovering over a large leather-work map spread across a table that took up nearly half the room.

"Excellent, you are all still awake," Adrik smiled at them, but there was no mirth in it. Truly, no one had seen any of the joviality that had previously been so easy and common for the dwarf since they arrived in Morabendar. "Brother Morgran informed us of the efficacy of his healing ritual, praise Othar. How is Erasmus?"

"Still resting," O'doc replied.

"As is to be expected," Adrik nodded, "and is doubtless in his best interests."

"Bearing that in mind, brother," Merida said, her eyes still on the map, "we'll need to account for his absence." She raised her head to look at Enna, O'doc, and Falken. "I am about to ask you all something, and I want nothing short of complete honesty." She waited a moment for their nods of assent, and continued. "I will be blunt: this attack on Deltharduin was unlike anything I have seen in all my years. We dwarves are no strangers to your arcana, and we have used our own rune-spells for as long as is known, but that creature was something altogether different. My brother has told me many times that you would be willing to aid Morabendar if asked, and he has told me of the strange things you have seen in the north. Under normal circumstances, I would stand by the fact that a matter amongst dwarves is best settled by dwarves alone, but it has become clear that something else is at work, and I am willing to do whatever is necessary to make sure whatever is threatening the thaneships, and all dwarves, is stopped."

"What would you have us do, milady?" Falken asked.

Merida pointed to a position on the map, a labrynthine diagram of tunnels and caverns. "This area here serves as the central way point between the thaneships. If Zanak marches an army toward Morabendar, it will inevitably pass through here. Supposing he's mobilized tonight, it should be roughly six days before he reaches the waypoint. It would take us three to do the same by gryphon, should we leave tonight."

"An ambush?" O'doc asked.

Merida nodded. "We are greatly outnumbered, especially after today's attack," she added. "The chance of our taking Zanak's army by surprise is the only advantage we have."

"What about the other thaneships?" Enna asked, looking to Adrik, who kept his eyes on the map. "People must have heard of Zanak's mysterious rise to power, and I'm sure if you approached the other thanes..."

"It would whittle away what precious time we have, milady." Adrik replied so quickly he practically cut the elf off.

"Not particularly," Falken offered, drawing paths over the map with his finger. "With how quickly those gryphons can travel, you could easily travel to the two nearer thaneships and back in a day.

Perhaps if each of you went with your own retinue, talked to the local thanes, we would still have time enough..."

"A useless effort and a waste of time," Merida cut the Professor off dismissively. "The southern thaneships were reluctant enough to deal with us in years past," she looked over at Adrik, "never mind trying to ally with them now."

"What do you mean by that?" Enna asked, evidently taking offense to the pointed jab at Adrik.

"That is none of your concern, Summerlark," Merida replied testily. "Now, can we continue discussing the plan?"

"We *are* discussing the plan," Enna contested. "You said you needed our help, and when we offer it you, wave it away like this."

"If you truly wish to help, girl," Merida began, evidently becoming aggravated, "then you'll sit down, listen to what I tell you, and act according to my orders."

"Your orders," Enna's eyes narrowed as she affixed them on Merida's, "are going to get us all killed." The elf's gaze moved between Merida and Adrik, the latter of the two avoiding it. "I know you're not telling us everything, and I, for one, have no interest in trusting people who don't care to trust me." Adrik's eyes briefly caught Enna's in that moment, and he saw in them the bitter look of disappointment.

"Fine then," Merida glared at Enna. "You can take your damned owls and fly back to the north. I've no place in my ranks for some cocky fae-folk bitch..."

"Enough, Merida!" Adrik cut his sister short, finally meeting Enna's gaze eye-to-eye, a look of defeat coming through the purple tinge of his own. "These are my friends, they deserve to know everything..." The dwarf took a long, deep breath, looking at each of his three companions in the room before he continued. "I am afraid that Morabendar's dearth of allies is a direct result of choices I made long ago..."

"I was young, brash, and heartbroken," Adrik's eyes looked down through the map as he continued, his stare now years away. "Her name was Beylatria... Beyla. She was a smith's daughter from Rimfil to the south, working a wench job in a tavern here in Deltharduin I happened to be particularly fond of. She was beautiful, witty, adventurous... our courtship was quick." He smiled wistfully as he recounted the memories. "More than anything, I loved that she knew who I was, and loved me neither because nor in spite of it. My station was of no consequence. I can remember her telling me once, 'when we are apart, I serve drunks and you serve subjects, but when we are together that matters not, for all we serve then is one another.'"

His smile faded as he continued. "My father was hardly enthused by the romance, going as far as to forbid my bringing Beyla to court. I had often avoided court prior, and with Beyla in my life and my father's decrees, the embers of my dissent were stoked only further. It was not long before she was with child... I was elated, though the news only served to drive a wedge further between myself and my father." Adrik shook his head slowly, speaking in a somber, lamenting tone. "He was not a cruel man, I have come to realize. His was a delicate position, and in his eyes I doubtless seemed an impulsive, arrogant youth, willing to compromise our family's name on a youthful tryst that would only end in heartbreak, or perchance on conniving individuals vying for a way to slither into noble standing."

"My father began to find reasons for me to stay away from Beyla, looking for courtly duties that could have easily been attended to by a page, and though it pained me to be away from my love, the mother of my child, I had hoped that perhaps assenting to these tasks might mend what had been cleft between myself and my father, possibly leading to his acceptance of Beyla." Adrik's voice began to strain, each sentence harder to deliver than the last. "I was not there when she was giving birth. The child was early, months early, and I was inundated with my duties. I received word from the nursemaid who attended her that evening. She was so timid in her approach, so I knew she bore ill tidings. The old woman explained to me that the babe was stillborn, dead before he left the womb. The labour was long, and rife with complications. Beyla..." the dwarf's voice audibly cracked, and he cast his eyes downward to hide the tears welling within them. "The struggle of it... she did not survive."

He laughed, a short, curt laugh used to stifle the sobs that hid beneath it. "The poor nursemaid looked so worried as she delivered the news, as though she feared I might strike her. Instead I did nothing. I was numb, as though my soul were stricken from my body. I thanked her and walked away in a trance. Finally, I came upon the most secluded area I could find in the whole of Citadel Moraben, and I fell to the ground and wept. I wept mournfully for the loss of the most precious things in my life, and I wept angrily for my inability to be there, my complete impotence in the situation."

"Naturally, my blame ricocheted off myself and found purchase in my father. I cursed him as I lay on the cold floor of that secluded room, and I cursed every damnable drop of noble blood in my body. I left that night, speaking not a word to anyone. When I parted your company in East Fellowdale that night, it was on the news that my father had passed. I had managed to stay so out of reach of the Otharines, however, that the news reached me years after the fact. The void left in his absence and mine strained our relations to the other thaneships, irreparably, I fear." The dwarf was quiet a moment longer before adding, as though it had just occurred to him, "I was never able to make my peace with him..."

Enna walked over to the dwarf, tears in her own eyes, and placed a hand on his shoulder. "Oh Adrik, why did you never tell us any of this?"

Adrik chuckled low, dabbing his violet eyes with one of his gloved hands. "When we four ventured out from your homestead, milady, we had nary known one another a fortnight! What's more, I had wanted nothing more than to leave Morabendar behind, and I was finally able to see that escape in you lot, and our quest to ascertain your origins." He smiled at the elf, looking up at her. "You were the first true companions I had in longer than I can say, and I did not want to burden you with the ghosts of an old dwarf's past."

"Well I fear you may have botched that spectacularly, friend," a familiar voice, if laden with pain and fatigue, spoke from the doorway. Erasmus Stonehand, keeping himself upright with the aid of Brother Morgran, stood in the stone threshold. "You mind telling me why you keep revealing all your secrets when I'm not around, Adrik?"

The dwarf walked around the table and toward the door. "Because the last thing I need is a gods-be-damned bard using my tragedy to line his own purse." He smiled through his beard, now a mess of half-wound braids, and clasped the half-elf's hand before pulling him into a tight hug. "Thank Othar you aren't dead, friend."

Erasmus stood back and placed his hands on Adrik's shoulders. "Now, it seems you've got yourself in a bit of a conundrum."

"Indeed." Adrik sighed. "We are on the brink of invasion, underpowered, and without a single ally. Our only hope..."

"Is not to meet the Ulbaryn army head-on," Erasmus finished, looking back at Merida. "Apologies, milady, but I'm inclined to agree with Enna. That plan will not end well."

"And I gather you've got a better one?" Merida asked, more than a hint of incredulity in her voice.

"Not yet, but I'm working on it." Erasmus replied. "What we need to do is slow Zanak's approach. The best bet for that is stealth." The bard turned his gaze to O'doc. "Lucky for you all, you've got the best smugglers in the Four Kingdoms at your disposal."

Chapter 21

Headmaster Daylen Cresthill sat alone in the plush cab of the coach that was taking him from Frostpoint to Heavenguard. He would have still been in awe of the fact that he had twice now used that strange chamber to travel from one coast of the Kingdoms to the other so effortlessly, but his mind was otherwise occupied, abuzz with the news he was to bring his queen. A pack that held a number of books and scrolls sat next to the Headmaster. Some were old and delicate, wrapped in layers of sheepskin for protection, while others were as recent as the last month, scrawled notes by Professor Coldstone. The man was a doubtless genius, as Cresthill was able to tell from the piles of research he had spent days sifting through. Sifting was putting the matter lightly, he thought. The Coldstone manor was a disaster. Were it not for the elf woman Zarah helping him organize everything, there was little chance he'd have made his discovery. If the Professor's mind was even half as cluttered as his house, it was no mystery how he'd not come to the realization himself sooner.

Zarah had accompanied him, largely at Lannister's behest, claiming he had 'personal matters' to attend to. She had opted to sit with the coachman, keeping an eye on the road, despite the Headmaster's claim that there were no roads as safe as those in Lohvast. Cresthill's thoughts halted with the coach. Peering through the curtains out the side window, he could see that they had stopped early and were still on the road. Unsure of what was going on, but fearing little more than a uncooperative horse, the Headmaster stepped out from the coach, only to be met with a crude cudgel as it swung from somewhere beside him and made contact to the side of his head, causing him to reel and fall over sideways.

The ringing in the Headmaster's ears from the blow had not even ceased as he felt himself being dragged toward the front of the coach and tossed on the ground next to Zarah and the coachman, both bound at the wrists and ankles. "I thought you were keeping an eye on the road," he said groggily, turning his head to the elf.

"There are three of them, and they ambushed us," she replied with a hoarse, testy whisper. "They came out of nowhere, I think one of them might be an arcanist."

"That's a ridiculous notion," Cresthill answered back as he regained his wits. "We're in the middle of Lohvast. No self-respecting arcanist here would waste their talents on petty banditry." Two sleight figures, one presumably the one who had struck the Headmaster, grabbed the fur-trimmed

172

scruff of his cloak and pulled him to his feet. Walking toward the front of the coach was a third. All three of the coach's attackers wore skins and cloaks dyed hues of gray and white, befitting camouflage in the wintery Lohvastine regions, Cresthill noted. Their hoods were pulled up and their faces concealed but for the eyes, revealing nothing of who or what they could be.

The third figure, presumably the trio's leader, looked at Cresthill a moment, before looking to either of the figures holding him. "Thirya, Lorak, tangwa-narda' i' edan." The voice was female, speaking Elvish. The two figures proceeded to bind the headmaster at the wrists, but left him standing. The leader approached Cresthill, speaking now in the Common tongue. "Who do you serve?"

"Her Grace, Queen Merrian Arkalis of Lohvast," the headmaster responded indignantly. "I do not know who you are, but you are interfering with a direct agent of her Grace on official matters. Untie us and let us be on our way, and I'll not speak a word of this to her Grace."

The woman closed the distance between she and Cresthill, grasping his chin and pulling it down so as to look deeply into his eyes. Her own eyes offered little, save that she was intently staring into the Headmaster's gaze, as though she were searching for something. "Aithen." she said simply, adding "Gul." Still clasping the Headmaster's chin, her eyes still affixed to his, the woman reached into the folds of her cloak with her free hand, and drew from its folds an amulet. Holding it tight, Cresthill could hear the faintest muffled whisper from behind the woman's mask. Though he could not make out the spell she was casting, the Headmaster began to feel strange, as though he were rousing from a dream he did not realize he was having. His mind began to wander back to his last meeting with Queen Merrian. She had called him a "wise tactician"... no... she had said something else... his head throbbed as he tried to recount what she had said, the sight of her mouth moving in his mind's eye, but straining to understand the words it formed.

In an instant, Cresthill was thrust back into the present, as he felt himself thrust to the ground, next to the bodies of the two that had bound him, their throats neatly slit. The Headmaster rolled away in surprise and horror and scrambled to his feet, looking over to see Zarah, daggers in either hand, about to attack the woman, who was positioned in such a way as was evident that she meant to cast a spell.

Realizing that his staff was still in the coach, leaving him unable to cast, the Headmaster charged toward the distracted woman, knocking her to the ground with a tackle. Rolling away just in time, Cresthill watched as Zarah pounced on their assailant, pining her to the ground, plunging both daggers deep into her chest, and holding them there until the masked woman no longer moved. The hood of the now dead woman's cloak had fallen off in the scuffle, revealing long black hair pulled back into a neat bun, and long, pointed ears.

"What in the hells were a group of elves doing ambushing a coach in the middle of Lohvast?" Cresthill asked, as much to himself as to Zarah. The throbbing in his head had subsided, as had the strange waking feeling.

"Damned if I know." Zarah cleaned her blades and cut the headmaster free, proceeding to do the same to the still evidently stunned coachman.

"You couldn't understand what they were saying?" Cresthill wrung his sore, unbound wrists with his hands.

"I was an orphan who grew up on whatever Ghestal streets I wasn't recognized in," she replied matter-of-factly. "No sense in learning anything past the Common speech, and whatever else would keep me alive, like how to get out of bonds, for instance." She looked at the coachman. "Are you hurt?"

"No, milady," he shook his head.

"Good. We'll need to make haste for Heavenguard," the elf's eyes scanned the area suspiciously. "I've got a feeling this war of Queen Merrian's is having an effect on the safety of the roads." She motioned for the Headmaster to help her with one of the bodies. "No time to bury them," she said as they picked one up, "but best not to leave them in the open for people to see."

"What do you think they wanted?" Cresthill asked as they carried the body well off the road.

"Whose to say?" she shrugged. "All I know is that whatever this big discovery of yours is, we'd best get it a far away from these roads as we can, and quick."

Chapter 22

Caliope Hollowpot woke up dazed and disoriented. Her shoulder throbbed, and she felt dizzy and nauseous. As she tried to recall what happened, her head began to pound in time with her shoulder. She was heading towards the Professor's manor, in part to make sure he was safe, and in part to chide him for worrying her so. The halfling shook her head lamely, and as her vision started to regain focus, she began to recognize her surroundings. She was in the Professor's manor, in his kitchen. Before she could ask herself any of the questions racing through her mind, though, Caliope noticed that she was not alone. She was tied to a chair at one side of the small wooden table her friend kept in the kitchen, at the other side of which sat another halfling, one whom Caliope did not recognize, and whose sly-eyed gaze caused her stomach to churn more heavily than it already was.

"Fantastic," the other halfling said to her as he saw her coming to. "You woke faster than I hoped."

"Who... are you?" Caliope asked groggily, annoyed that she hadn't the wits about her to say something more useful.

"Strange as it may sound, my sweet," the other halfling grinned, "I'm someone who's just become closer to you than anyone else ever will in your life." He hopped off his chair and bowed low. "I am Lannister Ravenclaw, guildmaster of the River Rats, Security Advisor to Queen Merrian of Lohvast, and devoted servant of the Mission."

Caliope shook her head slowly, the memory of the moments before she blacked out slowly seeping back into her consciousness. "The... River Rats..." she repeated slowly, feeling the stinging of an open wound on her back. Her eyes widened, and her realization sobered her up as quickly as it caused a wave of nausea to wash over her. She looked up at Lannister, glaring at him. "So then I'm..." she could not bring herself to say it, but the other halfling's sickly smirk confirmed her suspicion. "Why would you? I've no business with your lot, nor would I ever wish to."

"That, my sweet, is where you're wrong," Lannister began to pace slowly and casually about the kitchen, absentmindedly picking at some grapes sitting on the table. "You see, I happen to have a penchant for the gathering of information. It's a bit of an obsession, really." He popped a grape into his mouth, audibly chewing as he continued. "It's such an obsession, that if someone, let's say a local priestess, had some information that I didn't, well then, I may be inclined to use whatever means I have to gain that information."

"I have no idea what you think I know." Caliope replied, trying ineffectually to struggle out of her bonds. "But even if I did have some kind of information you needed, did you truly expect that you could draw it from me by kidnapping me and..." she hesitated, fighting the urge to vomit, "...infecting me?"

Lannister hopped onto the table and let loose a chuckle as he continued to chew on the grapes. "Here I'd assumed that a learned woman like yourself would know a few things about lycanthropes," he shook his head in mock pity. "So few take the time to really understand us. For instance," he began, turning his head and staring deep into Caliope's eyes. His gaze bore into her, and try as she might, she was unable to look away. "Did you know that a lycanthrope shares a special bond with whoever turned them?" Caliope began to feel all the hairs on her body stand on end. "So special, in fact, that we can only turn one other person."

The hairs on Caliope's body began to thicken, and she sat horrified and confused as she felt her physical features begin to change, and was unable to do anything but stare into the jaundiced eyes in front of her.

"I remember the girl who turned me. Another of the Rats, her name was Millie. She was my mentor, my lover. She wanted to run the Rats more than anyone else I knew, except maybe me." He laughed, reminiscing. "She taught me how to half-change, then made me kill our guildmaster in his sleep." He leaned in close to Caliope, and she could feel his breath. "Before she could take her place at the head of the Rats, I did the same to her."

Caliope fought the urge to scream as her transformation came to an end. Her hands and feet slipped from their bonds, and she stood up, though not of her own volition. Though she was aware of her thoughts, she was unable to act accordingly, feeling instead like she was in the midst of a dream. She looked down at her now hair-covered hands, and looked about to see that she was slightly shorter, and her clothing now sat loose upon her, and though she felt a sickness course through her mind, she felt nothing manifest physically.

"Fantastic, isn't it?" Lannister beamed. "Now, let's see how well this works. Tell me your full name, sweet."

The halfling could hear herself answer, "Caliope Loremite Hollowpot."

"Very good. Now, my sources tell me that you have a connection to someone I'm looking for." A sinister smile played across Lannister's face. "How do you know O'doc Overhill?"

Caliope's mind screamed in protest, but to no avail. "I am his aunt, sister of his Mother, Ornella Overhill."

"Family?" Lannister mused. "Oh, that makes this all the better. Alright, now tell me, where is the little bastard?"

"I do not know." Caliope said with some relief.

"You don't know?" Lannister's annoyance was visible. "My sources say they spotted him in this very manor, and that you escorted him here."

"That is true."

"So how in the hells did you manage to lose him?"

"I had not heard from O'doc, nor his friends, in several days." Caliope responded. "I was coming to Professor Coldstone's manor to check on them when you found me." With any luck, Caliope thought, Lannister would realize she was a dead end. She saw him pondering, and felt herself go cold when he asked his next question.

"Does O'doc's mother live in East Fellowdale?" his crooked grin flashed.

"No, she lives at the Overhill Homestead in Khalen Ridge."

He nodded, satisfied. "Alright, Caliope, I need you to escort me to Khalen Ridge, to the Overhill's home."

Caliope Hollowpot, acting against the voice screaming dissent within her mind, stood up. She became painfully aware of her reduced height and raised senses, of the coarse fur that now covered her body, and of the tail that now dragged along the ground as she walked. As Caliope stepped out into the dark streets of the East Fellowdale night, she wished to weep, but could not. Her actions were Lannister's to control, and so the priestess did the only thing for which she had the free will, and prayed silently as she methodically made her way to Khalen Ridge.

Chapter 23

A pair of large gryphons plodded gently through the main arterial tunnel-way from the Morabendine outskirts toward Otharbund, a colossal expanse of caverns that serves as the main waypoint between the Dwarven Thaneships. The gryphons pulled a small stonework wagon behind them, upon which sat Merida Mettlehelm and Enna Summerlark. They had been the last to leave Deltharduin. Erasmus and O'doc had left almost immediately after the group had settled on a plan the evening prior, the half-elf waving off Brother Morgran's protestations with a lopsided smirk, and the promise that he and O'doc would 'stay out of trouble,' a statement that none of the others wholly believed, but forced themselves to under the circumstances.

Adrik and Falken set out the next morning. While neither Merida nor Adrik were particularly optimistic about a dishonoured thane taking a human to speak with him in the southern Thaneships, Merida knew her place was with the Morabendine army, and Adrik understood that the Professor's grasp of Dwarfish might prove as a useful diplomatic asset for them.

Enna had set out with Merida that evening, riding ahead as the full force of the Morabendine army marched behind them, their measured steps echoing off the tall tunnel ceilings. The dwarf had said little since they left Deltharduin, and the elf even less. Much occupied Enna's mind as the two rode along. She worried that Erasmus had not healed well enough, and that he might compromise he and O'doc's role in their plan, or that conversely, the plan might compromise the still-wounded half-elf's well-being. She worried that the southern Thanes would be unreceptive, or possibly hostile toward Adrik and Falken. She worried that, even if her friends were all successful in their efforts, time was not on their side, and that the Ulbar army would easily outmatch them.

Enna's worries were made none the more easy by the presence of Merida Mettlehelm. The dwarf's stoic, gruff disposition was so unlike her brother's, and so much more stern and serious than anyone with whom Enna had ever associated. The few times Merida had spoken since they left involved mostly shouting back at one of her captains. She said nothing to Enna, and seemed not to be bothered that Enna had said nothing to her.

For what seemed like hours, little changed for Enna. The tunnel-way seemed to stretch onward, each expanse so like the last that she would have thought they had been traveling in circles. Eventually, the elf felt her eyes begin to get heavy, the long, monotonous journey beginning to weigh on her. Fighting to stay awake, for fear that Merida would take offense to her dozing off, the elf was suddenly roused back into full alertness by the sudden stoppage of the cart, combined with the baritone caws of the gryphons as they were pulled to a halt.

"We're here," Merida said ineffectually, hopping off the cart to tie off the gryphons. "Start setting up camp."

Enna climbed down her side of the wagon and looked around. The light had dimmed, not for lack of the runelamps that marked the walls of so much of the Dwarven land, but because the area in which they had stopped was so immense that the elf had to strain her eyes to see the faintest glints of light along the nearest cave walls. The cavern ceilings were so tall that Enna could only just barely make out the tips of the lowest hanging stalactites, descending forebodingly from the shadows above. Straining to see anything, Enna drew forth her club, touching one hand to the head of it, and uttered, *"KALINA."* A soft light sprung forth from the head of the club, and Enna replaced it in her belt, walking toward the back of the wagon to gather the supplies to make camp.

"Lord and scions, what do you think you're doing?" Merida barked as Enna walked toward her with armfuls of supplies. "Put that damned fae-light out!"

"But I can't see where I'm going without it!" Enna protested, laying the supplies on the ground. "I'm not a dwarf."

"Indeed no, but everybody else within several miles is." Merida retorted, shielding her eyes from the light. "Including the Ulbar army, and something that bright will make our position known faster than a miner can find an opal."

Enna sighed resignedly, and touched her hand to her club head, dispelling the glow. "Well I'm not sure what you'd like me to do, then."

"Can you see well enough to build a fire?"

Enna nodded.

"Well build it, then. It's all you'll need for the time."

Soon enough, camp had been properly set up, and Enna warmed herself by the small fire she'd made, opting to cast a spell to light the blaze, both for expedience and practice. The fireball spell did not weaken her as much as it had in past weeks, but it did still send a terrible chill through her. Coupled with the chill of the cavern, she wrapped herself in her thick fur cloak as she sat by the campfire.

Merida walked up to the campfire, her heavy armour removed in favour of a thick wool tunic and pants. She carried two steaming bowls, and handed one to Enna. "Eat," she said simply. "You'll need it."

"Thank you." Enna took one bowl and smiled courteously as Merida sat next to her. It was a plain stew of root vegetables, not particularly flavourful, but hearty and warm nonetheless.

"Get that chill out of your bones." Merida said, not looking up at Enna as she ate her own stew. "You'll not be much good in battle if you're shivering like a shaved goat."

The pair sat by the fire and ate in silence for some time, while Enna thought about the impending battle. Finally, she looked up and stared into the fire. "You've killed before, haven't you Lady Merida?"

The dwarf looked into the dancing flames as well, and nodded solemnly after a moment "I'd likely not be of my station if I hadn't." Her response was simple and to-the-point, and reminded Enna of the tone O'doc had taken with her those weeks ago after he had killed the two goblins. "I take it you've not, Summerlark?"

Enna slowly shook her head. "Chickens and rabbits, and the like, but never something with a mind. I don't..."

"Know if you can?" Merida finished. "You just do. If you have to take a life to keep your own, you find you don't think twice about it."

"How?" Enna asked. "How do you push it from your mind?"

"You don't," Merida answered. She loosed a short, mirthless chuckle. "Whenever you hear the bards' songs, any time a great hero is slain, they sing about the light leaving their eyes. It's a myth, you know. When you see someone take their last breath, there's no light being extinguished. Those eyes stay as bright as they were in life, and more often than not they look straight into yours as they fall. I wish I could tell you that there's some kind of spell or prayer to make it all go away, but the truth of the matter is those eyes stay with you, and one day you realize you've seen so many of them that you can't tell one set from the next, and that you've ended enough lives that one more won't make it any harder to sleep."

The two sat in silence once again, but this time, as Merida gazed into the fire, Enna looked over at the dwarf. Enna no longer saw Merida's gruffness, but instead saw the dwarf's surly disposition as something that hung over top her, as though it were clothing or armour that had been carefully tailored over the years, sitting so snug over her that one would be hard pressed to see it for what it was.

Finally, Merida stood. "I'd best be heading back to my own camp. The gods know Morgran's likely wondering where I've gone." She walked over to Enna, and reached into a fold in her tunic. "Speaking of the old fool, I told him about your mucking about with fae-light, had him make this so you won't be so stupid twice." She drew forth a pendant of simple stone strung along a length of leather. Carved into the stone were a series of runes that Enna could not make out.

"Oh!" she said in genuine surprise. "Thank you, Lady Merida."

"Just Merida, Summerlark, or Commander Mettlehelm on the field. And thank Morgran, not me." She began to walk into the darkness. "Get some sleep, Summerlark, you'll be no good to me if you're quivering and exhausted."

As Merida slipped into the darkness of the cavern, Enna tied the necklace around her neck. As soon as the pendant fell across her breast, she felt a strange, warm feeling emanating through her, akin to what she felt when casting spells, only flowing into her, rather than from her. When she looked around, Enna was shocked at what she saw. It was as though the cavern had been illuminated, like light was pouring into it from some unknown source. She looked up and saw the cavern ceiling, at least two hundred feet up, and the walls, miles apart at their widest point. Looking out toward the other camps, Enna saw Morgran Mettlehelm greeting his wife with a kiss, and smiled, knowing that there was more to Merida Mettlehelm than the armour she wore, even if Enna only ever got that small glimpse beneath it.

Chapter 24

The journey from Deltharduin was slower-going than Erasmus and O'doc would have liked. While they had opted to travel on foot, favouring discretion over speed, they lost time in Otharbund, keeping to the light-paneled walls of the cavern rather than risking the darkness of the cavern's centrepoint. Travel sped up for the pair once they reached the opposite end of the cavern, however, returning to the relatively well-lit cave systems to which they had become accustomed in the past weeks. Erasmus had little trouble traveling, much to O'doc's relief, but every so often the half-elf showed signs that he still had not fully recovered from his injuries.

Roughly four days into their journey, the pair began to come across Ulbar dwarves, occasional scouts no doubt surveying the path to Morabendar. O'doc and Erasmus opted to not make camp that evening, instead pressing on in stealth by following one of the scouts. The dwarf made little effort to be discreet on the way back from his reconnaissance, no doubt assured that the way was clear, making it that much easier for the two sell-swords to follow him back to camp.

The dwarf camp consisted of five sheepskin tents dyed blue and black, the colours of Ulbaryn, O'doc surmised. Cooking fires cast dancing shadows along the cave walls, and a raucous affair could be heard very distinctly from one tent above the others, noticeably also the tent the scout retreated to. The halfling and half-elf exchanged a knowing glance, and proceeded to creep toward the tent, doing their best to remain among the tall shadows that adorned the cave walls.

The pair made their way to the outside wall of the tent nearest the majority of the firelight, ensuring they would be under as much cover of darkness as possible. Crouching down, O'doc reached down to the sheath on his left hip and drew a dagger, proceeding to slowly, and carefully cut a slit roughly three inches long down the sheepskin. The halfling let out a short breath of relief at the realization that the skin was not pulled so taut as to cause the incision to split further than necessary.

Closing one eye and peeking into the hole, O'doc looked around as best he could to survey the tent's interior. It had clearly been set up as some manner of mess hall, as through his limited range of view O'doc could see several dwarves in differing amounts of armour sitting at tables where they ate and drank. In the corner of his view range, the halfling spotted the scout he and Erasmus had tailed to the camp, speaking with an older dwarf, whose scarred face was in stark contrast to his bright blue eyes and white beard and hair. Even when the din within the tent died down, and O'doc strained his ears, however, he was not able to make out what the two were saying.

"No use," he whispered hoarsely to his partner, still staring through the hole, attempting to read the dwarves' lips. "I think they're speaking Dwarfish... what do you think we should do?"

A gruff voice answered back in Dwarfish, as O'doc felt the point of what was likely a dagger at the back of his neck. The halfling cursed under his breath as he slowly raised his hands, placing them behind his head as he methodically stood up and turned around. A dwarf faced him, holding up what was, indeed, a dagger, that was now pointed squarely at his Adam's apple. A quick glance revealed that another guard clasped a gauntlet-clad hand across the mouth of the still kneeling half-elf, while her own dagger sat in wait just below his chin. The look in Erasmus' eyes was more one of annoyance than any semblance of worry. Erasmus and O'doc allowed themselves to be bound at the wrists, and proceeded to be marched at knife-point toward the entrance of the tent.

The cacophony of voices inside the tent ceased almost instantly as Erasmus and O'doc walked through the tent flaps and into the midst of roughly thirty dwarves, most of whom now bore an expression between surprise at the unexpected visitors, and annoyance that their revelry had been interrupted. The older, scarred dwarf O'doc had spied earlier walked slowly past the others, intensely examining the half-elf and halfling. The dwarf looked to the two who had captured Erasmus and O'doc, and spoke briefly with both of them in Dwarfish before returning his eyes to the two intruders, addressing them in the slow, calculated speech of one not using their native tongue. "Who sent you here?"

O'doc looked at the old dwarf, discreetly studying his face. There was suspicion in his expression, but not the surprise evident in the faces of the dwarves in his command. This dwarf, O'doc reasoned, knew something the others did not, and the halfling would suss out what that information was. "You weren't expecting us, then?" he said, hoping the answer was vague enough to draw more from the old dwarf.

The dwarf's eyes narrowed. "Our Thane was not clear? Or you did not get message?" A cursory glance of the rest of the tent assured O'doc that none of the other dwarves could understand common speech.

Erasmus, beginning to catch onto what his partner was doing, stepped in. "We should speak somewhere private," he motioned his head past the old dwarf. "Your men and women want food and drink after a long day, do not let us interrupt them."

The dwarf looked at the two a moment longer, his expression unclear as to whether he was considering Erasmus' words, or simply trying to understand them. Finally, he nodded, and turned to face the rest of the tent. He spoke something in Dwarfish, and the resultant cheers from the rest of the tent caused Erasmus and O'doc to exchange worried sidelong glances. The dwarf faced the two once more, saying only, "follow," before passing between the two of them, and motioning their captors to keep them within their grasp.

The group walked through the camp before reaching a smaller tent, its interior better furnished than the last. The old dwarf walked to the opposite end of a small table at the tent's far end, and muttered something to the guards. The one holding Erasmus began to speak, presumably in protest, but was quickly silenced by the old dwarf, who repeated himself. The two guards proceeded to release Erasmus and O'doc from their bindings. The old dwarf turned around to face them, producing two stone mugs full of what appeared to be ale, and motioned to a pair of stools at the opposite side of the table. "Sit," he said simply, placing the mugs in front of the seats. When neither O'doc nor Erasmus were quick to seat themselves, the dwarf chuckled. "If I want Lohvast spies dead, I not poison. I just make Bemvik and Sarna..." he pointed to the two guards, and then dragged his thumb across his throat. He motioned once more to the stools. "Sit."

The pair did so, tentatively, as the old dwarf produced a frothing mug of his own. He held the mug out to toast. "To friendship of Ulbaryn and Lohvast." O'doc and Erasmus joined in the toast, only just sipping at their ales as the dwarf took a long

draught of his own. "I am not sure why you are here,"
the dwarf said finally, wiping the foam from his
beard.

"Well, Lohvast and Ulbaryn are such good
friends..." O'doc began, hoping the toast was more
than a formality.

"They are," the dwarf nodded. "Long years of
trade." He pointed a stubby finger back and forth at
the pair. "But friends do not spy on friends."

"We were only taking orders." Erasmus offered
in as apologetic a tone as possible. "When the queen
heard whispers of war..."

The dwarf spat onto the ground next to him.
"Bah! The new queen..." he shook his head. "The new
queen has her own war to worry over." The dwarf
refilled his mug, drinking once more. "This new
queen, I do not like... Old king and queen were strong
and fair, this new queen..." the dwarf made a motion
as though he were holding a large, heavy object on
both hands, testing its weight, "she wants much, will
do much for it..."

"And yet here you are, on the eve of war
yourself," Erasmus countered.

The dwarf chuckled knowingly. "Your queen
has army of arcanists, no?"

The pair nodded slowly, trying to mask the
fact that this was news to them.

The dwarf nodded in return, a knowing smile
peeking through his beard. "I do not think you like
war, but two men are not army of arcanists, and I
think you like life." Another long drink. "I do not like

war, but I am one dwarf, and Thane Zanak moves stone." He looked at Erasmus and O'doc, self-satisfied. "I am old because I like life more than I do not like war."

There was a long pause, silence enveloping the tent completely, before being shattered by the sound of the dwarf's mug being slammed onto the tabletop.

"I let you go," he told the pair with a grin. "Do not want Lohvast blood on Ulbar hands. Bemvik and Sarna take you to northwest Otharines, then you tell your queen Zanak has war of his own, and will not help."

Erasmus and O'doc stood and bowed to the dwarf. "You're a most gracious host," the halfling said. "We would pass word along to the queen of the one who showed us such hospitality, if only we had your name."

The dwarf chuckled once more. "Not best spies. Did not learn my name. I not give you, either. I give my name, better spies could find me." He snapped to the two dwarves who had found O'doc and Erasmus, and motioned them over to the pair, where they proceeded to bind the half-elf and halfling's hands once more. "Must be careful," the dwarf offered apologetically.

"Of course," Erasmus smirked and bowed his head. "We'll not resist."

Erasmus and O'doc were led out of the tent by the two guards, the older dwarf walking back toward the larger tent as they exited. "Safe travels, spies. May Othar see you home safe, and never back in Ulbaryn."

The dwarf said one last thing to the guards in Dwarfish before he departed, and the guards began to march their captives further into the tunnels.

The dwarves, armed now with short swords, marched Erasmus and O'doc away from the camp for some time, with little but the occasional runelamp lighting the way, bright enough to signify that it was still late afternoon. The trek had become so monotonous, with none involved uttering so much as a word since their departure, that O'doc almost did not notice the distinct lack of a sword tip pressing into his back. Nor did any of the others notice, until Erasmus and his captor stopped abruptly, the dwarf spinning on her heels to see her partner several tens of feet behind them, taking a long drink from a water skin. She yelled something in Dwarfish, the annoyance apparent in her voice. The other dwarf answered back in kind, prompting the first to begin a shouting match. Her argument was interrupted, however, as Erasmus used the distraction to charge into her, throwing his shoulder between her shoulder blades and knocking her to the ground, and throwing himself atop her.

O'doc, seeing the second dwarf begin to charge toward them, began to run toward the dwarf. The dwarf held his sword over his head with both hands, planning to swing downward and cleave the halfling. As the dwarf's blade came down, O'doc tumbled to the side, throwing his attacker off balance. The halfling kicked the back of the dwarf's knee, causing it to buckle and the dwarf to fall. As the dwarf attempted to stand back up and face the halfling, O'doc quickly slipped his bound wrists under his tucked legs and sprang up, meeting the dwarf with a fierce two-handed swing directly up into his jaw. The dwarf, dazed by the unexpected hit, made no effort to block the successive swings across either cheek, the latter of the two causing him to stumble and collapse, unconscious.

O'doc picked up the dwarf's short sword with both hands and walked over to Erasmus, who still laid atop the still conscious dwarf, no longer struggling at the sight of the halfling holding the blade. "Help me tie her up, will you?" Erasmus bade his partner. "I may be taller, I can't hold her much longer on my own."

The halfling cut Erasmus loose, and proceeded to hold the sword out at the dwarf as the half-elf rummaged through their packs, finding a length of rope with which he bound the dwarf. He then used one of O'doc's daggers to cut his bindings, leaving the dwarves where they were as they ran back from whence they had come.

The pair ran for some time before allowing themselves a moment to rest, their breaths heavy as they both took a moment to lay their backs along a cave wall.

"So what now?" O'doc asked, panting.

Erasmus shook his head, equally winded. "I don't know, but I think we need to head closer to Ulbaryn."

O'doc nodded. "I was afraid you'd say that." He took a few more heavy breaths. "What do you think that dwarf was talking about, about Lohvast starting a war?"

"I don't know..." Erasmus admitted, "but with our luck I've no doubt we'll find ourselves in the thick of it sooner rather than later."

Chapter 25

Adrik Thornmallet stood next to Falken, a cavern of near impenetrable darkness surrounded the pair and their mounts, save for the light cast from the arcanist's wand. "Tell me professor, as a learned individual, what do you know of the deep dwarves?"

Falken swallowed nervously as he looked around. "I must concede that I know less than I'd prefer."

"In truth, whatever you do know is likely more than they prefer." Adrik adjusted his tri-corn hat reflexively. "We dwarves of the northern mountains have, at worst, remained relatively amicable with the people of the Four Kingdoms. Our southern cousins, however..."

"Is it true what the bards' tales say? That they are blind? That they do not sleep?" Falken asked, his curiosity quickly followed by the embarrassment of asking such a juvenile string of questions.

Adrik let loose a quiet chuckle. "Tales grow in scope and fancy as they pass from one teller to the next." The dwarf looked sidelong at Falken. "I'm certain a man of your notoriety need not be told that."

Falken's face went hot, and he stared agog at the dwarf a moment. "I... suppose I needn't be surprised..." he stammered bitterly. "Anyone who's spent a fortnight in Ghest has likely been told some variant or the other."

"So what are its origins, then?" Adrik asked. "What was the true reason behind your disgrace?"

"Were that I knew myself..." Falken replied, half to himself. "The whole matter was so sudden, so unceremonious... I cannot help but feel as though my studies were somehow to blame."

"I cannot see how the study of the arcane would merit one's dismissal from an arcane university," Adrik reasoned, "unless one were attempting to toil with the dead, or some such nefarious deed."

"Nothing so dire," Falken smiled. "When I first began my tenure, my study focused on evocation, mostly on trying to better control the forces summoned by such a spell... a bit banal, academically speaking, but practical." He looked into the distance, searching for his memories within the blackness. "Then, I remember stumbling across something... I cannot recall what exactly, but at some point, I became compelled to understand the nature of arcana, the source. Everything I found was disjointed, however, or contradictory. It reached a point where I was not sleeping, between what I was required to research for the university, and what I was driven to seek in my own time... Headmaster Riverwall had caught wind of my... extracurriculars... and made it very clear that I was to focus squarely on my duties as a professor. By that point, I fear he was simply waiting for me to slip when..."

Adrik raised a hand to shush the man. "Apologies, Professor," he whispered hoarsely, "but I believe our parlay is at hand..."

The sound of something scraping against the ground could be faintly heard in the distance, interspersed with a distinct, rhythmic tapping that echoed off the walls and ceilings within the cavern.

"What is that noise?" Falken whispered, looking about the blackness in vain.

"They are surveying the area." Adrik answered in kind.

After a moment, the scraping and tapping ceased, replaced by the clicking of clawed feet, like those of a bear, growing increasingly close to Adrik and Falken. Eventually, the figures in the darkness made their way into the arcane light, causing Falken to gasp. From the impenetrable shadow emerged two colossal moles, each as big as any bear. Atop the moles were two dwarves; each pale skinned, with thick, knotted hair and beards, prominent ears, and small, beady eyes. Both had thick bone walking sticks at least five feet in length, and both wore some manner of animal skin clothing that, while well tailored, was simple and undyed. The dwarves stopped, and one looked back and forth at Adrik and Falken.

"Thane Adrik, I presume," the dwarf said after some time, speaking a dialect of Dwarfish that was so different from what Falken had ever heard that the professor was only able to make out part of what the deep dwarf said.

"You presume correctly," Adrik replied in his native dialect, "though I fear I am not acquainted with you, fine sir, nor your party."

"I am Glavik, this is Ruknym." the first deep dwarf motioned to the other. "We come on behalf of Thanes Malhor of Arvadem, and Harbans of Barkaan."

"And your retinue?" Adrik asked, leaving Falken to wonder how many of the dwarves lurked out of the reach of his arcane light.

"Their names are of little consequence at this moment," Ruknym stated flatly. "We note that you travel with little accompaniment yourself, Lord."

"Only with a trusted friend," Adrik coroborated.

"Professor Falken Coldstone, sirs, of the kingdom of Ghest," Falken bowed habitually, but in truth was unaware of whether or not the dwarves were able to see the gesture.

"The northerner speaks some Dwarfish," Glavik noted, surprise apparent in his voice. "A thane calling so abrupt an audience is not common, Lord," he continued, making little effort to mask the suspicion in his tone, "much less a thane who arrives on his own behalf, and with little but a northerner for protection."

"I come to you in a dire time," Adrik offered. "Since the untimely demise of the thane of Ulbaryn and the rise of his brother Zanak, there have been whispers that Ulbaryn aimed to make war with Morabendar. Several days ago Deltharduin was attacked outright, Citadel Moraben itself besieged upon. As we speak, the Morabendine army is fortifying ground at Otharbund, awaiting the inevitable march of Ulbaryn. I am personally requesting the aid of Arvadem and Barkaan in the defense of Morabendar."

"The northern thaneships have had their minor squabbles for centuries," Ruknym replied. "Through those centuries, Arvadem and Barkaan have never interceded, and we of the deeper Otharines are the better for it. This was a fact that your father knew well, Lord. Why do you waste your time and our own on a question for which you no doubt already know the answer?"

"This is not some minor squabble," Adrik retorted, maintaining his composure in spite of the deep dwarf's flippancy. "Thane Zanak possesses power the likes of which even the most powerful runemages have never seen. I saw first hand the destruction of Citadel Moraben at the hands of a great stone creature that would rival the giants of old. If Morabendar falls, I fear your homes will doubtless be next in Zanak's path."

"We have heard the rumors of Thane Zanak," Glavik nodded thoughtfully, "though in spite of them, there have been no untoward actions made against Arvadem, nor Barkaan."

"Should we ally ourselves with Morabendar, only to see it fall," added Ruknym, "then we would risk drawing the ire of Ulbaryn." The deep dwarf's voice was calculated and cold in the assertion. "It is a risk we cannot afford."

Adrik looked up at the two deep dwarves, his deep violet eyes catching Falken's light in such a way that their intensity shone. "While I've respect for your concerns, we have not the time to debate such matters in terms of hypotheticals," the dwarf took a deep breath. "I invoke the old law of Femrir Duul."

There was no visible reaction from either of the deep dwarves, save for Glavik slightly cocking his head in puzzlement. "You would call upon a law old as Othar himself? Challenge one of us to combat in exchange for a boon?"

"It is an old law," Adrik nodded. "Outdated at best, and barbaric at worst, but one we of the Otharines must recognize nonetheless. You leave me no choice."

Ruknym nodded, and with a fluidity of motion that belied his stocky frame and seemingly poor eyesight, dismounted his stout mole, and walked closer to Adrik and Falken, standing between the two. "I accept the challenge," he stated, his small eyes unmoving, "but not by your hands, Thane Adrik. I wish not to draw the ire of Morabendar should anything... unfortunate... transpire." The deep dwarf cocked his head slightly in the direction of Falken. "I accept on the terms that the northerner fight on your behalf."

"You cannot..." Adrik began to protest.

"He can," Glavik cut him off. "You have lain the challenge, so Ruknym may set the terms, such is the law."

"Perhaps the ways of his own people have been lost to him in the time he spent away from the Otharines," Ruknym called back to his companion. "Do not worry, Lord, declining my terms and withdrawing your challenge will not bring any more shame to clan Thornmallet than your absenteeism already begat."

"I will fight for the Thane," Falken interjected. He looked over to Adrik. The dwarf's eyes did not meet his, but the professor noted something in them that seemed almost like a look of relief.

"It is decided," Glavik stated matter-of-factly. "Challengers, you may each have a moment to prepare."

Falken looked to Adrik, who this time looked back. "Professor, I am speechless." he smiled, speaking now in the common tongue. "Such a selfless act is as unparalleled as ever I have seen."

"There was little choice in the matter, as far as I could see," Falken said passively. "Now, if you had any knowledge on deep dwarves that might be advantageous to me at this point..."

"Their eyesight is poor," Adrik answered quickly, "but their ancillary senses are all the better for it. Their ears are so keen, in fact, that they claim to hear the world around them better than any could ever see it."

The Professor nodded thoughtfully. "What do they know of arcana?"

"Little," Adrik replied. "Less even than the dwarves of the upper Otharines. They are aware of runemagery, but are generally hesitant to use it."

"Convenient," Falken said, half to himself. "Alright, I think I have an idea."

Adrik clapped Falken on the shoulder. "Best of luck, Professor. Othar's might be on your side."

Falken said nothing, simply keeping his eyes forward and nodding before walking toward Ruknym, who already stood in wait for the arcanist.

The two combatants stood roughly three feet from one another. The deep dwarf held a readied stance, gripping his walking stick in such a way that the staff evidently doubled as a weapon. Falken stood facing forward, hands at his sides, one in which he held the still-illuminated wand.

"The rules are simple," Glavik called out from atop his mole. "Combat ends when one of the combatants falls. If neither does so, then whomever willfully submits to the other accepts defeat. Understood?"

Both human and dwarf spoke their assent. There was a brief, still silence, where for a moment Falken looked into the small, dark eyes of his opponent, eyes that were not looking at anything in particular.

In a flash, Ruknym sprang into action, swinging his staff at the professor, who only barely jumped out of the way, feeling the rush of air brought forth by the speed of the attack. Completing the swing, the dwarf resumed a readied stance, tapping the top end of his staff to the ground twice.

Falken had to keep himself from tripping backward as he dodged the opening attack. The stumble caused his arms to fly wildly for a moment. His wand, his only source of light, began to swing about with equal abandon as a result, causing him to momentarily lose sight of his opponent, alerted to the dwarf's whereabouts only by the tapping of the staff against the stone floor of the cavern. The arcanist cursed his carelessness under his breath. He had not thought to cast a light spell onto anything else nearby, leaving him blind and vulnerable with even the slightest errant motion. He steadied himself and flashed his arcane light back at Ruknym, who had begun a charge toward the human, his staff raised in preparation for a downward swipe. Falken quickly stepped to the right of the swing, and the staff came down hard on the stone ground. Before the arcanist was able to prepare for another strike, he was taken unawares as the dwarf's staff slid along the ground, tripping Falken and causing him to hit the cold floor, his wand falling from his hand. The arcane light dispelled almost instantly, and Falken was met with blackness, and the feeling of Ruknym's staff, at his chin.

"I would think it in your best interests to submit, northerner." Ruknym said, smug satisfaction evident in his voice. "What say you?"

In that moment, Falken, who had been fumbling his hands about as best as he could in his current position, felt the smooth, familiar texture of his wand. Taking it in his right hand, and slowly, calmly placing his left hand upon the deep dwarf's staff, he closed his eyes, concentrated, and spoke.

"*KALINA!*"

In a sudden burst that was so bright Falken had to squint his already closed eyes, the deep dwarf cried out, and the professor heard the sound of the staff clattering onto the stone floor. He sprang up quickly to see the deep dwarf standing back from his staff, his eyes covered by his hands. The staff now pulsed with a bright white light that illuminated enough of the cavern that Falken could see at least a score of the dwarves crowded behind where Glavik sat atop his mount, many of them either gasping or covering their eyes.

Ruknym withdrew his hands from his face, his eyes still tightly closed. "A clever trick, northerner, but I do not need my eyes to defeat you..." The dwarf knelt down, picking up a loose rock, and threw it, only just missing the professor. "The stone speaks to me, northerner, and tells me where you are!"

Falken raised his wand in the direction of the deep dwarf and cried out, "*FEA OOMA!*" The professor watched as the dwarf charged toward him. Then, he spoke once more, this time channeling his voice now through his wand, and resounding it next to Ruknym, causing the dwarf to stop dead with a confused look on his face.

"The stone lies," the phantom voice spoke, causing Ruknym to swing wildly to his right flank, his fist finding no purchase. "Your ears are mine to command." The arcanist's voice appeared now to the dwarf's left flank, causing another wild swing into thin air.

"Cease your trickery, northerner!"

"Submit." The voice loomed behind the dwarf.

"I will not!" Ruknym spun on his heels and attempted to bear-hug the voice, the lack of physical presence resulting in the dwarf stumbling and falling, his beard the only cushion between his chin and the cold stone floor.

"Submit." The voice was calm and hanging over Ruknym.

"Stop this!" The frustration in the deep dwarf's voice was evident.

"Submit!" The voice took on a more stern tone, and hung closer to the dwarf as he turned onto his back.

"Stop!" Ruknym flailed his arms wildly, as if swatting at a swarm of flies. There was a hint of pleading, of panic evident now in the dwarf.

"SUBMIT!" the voice boomed loud enough to echo through the cavern, it's full intensity enveloping the deep dwarf.

"I submit!" Ruknym cried out, his hands covering his ears as he curled up on the ground. "I submit to you, please, just make the voice stop!"

In an instant, it was over. Falken let himself go limp, falling to one knee. Both the arcane spells dissipated, coating the cavern once more in impenetrable blackness. All that could be heard was the panting of the two combatants echoing through the otherwise still cavern.

"You are the victor, Falken Coldstone of the north." Glavik said finally, breaking the stillness. "Thane Adrik, we shall take your proposal to Arvadem and Barkaan. If able, we will assemble armies to aid you in your battle at Otharbund."

Adrik nodded solemnly. "You have my gratitude, Glavik. May the Lord and Scions see you home safely."

The deep dwarves said nothing else, instead simply collecting themselves and turning back from whence they came. Falken, having rested for a minute, conjured another small light on his wand, and began to walk back toward Adrik.

"Professor Coldstone, that was the single most magnificent display of arcana I have..." Adrik did not continue, as the arcanist simply passed him with neither word nor eye contact, walking directly over to one of the gryphons the pair took to the meeting, and mounting it.

Adrik walked over and did the same with the second gryphon, choosing not to try speaking to Falken again. Instead, the pair rode through the expanses of tunnels in silence. It was not until they began to see the faintest glow of runelamps that the silence was finally broken.

"Did you know they would choose me to fight?" the professor asked plainly, his eyes remaining ahead.

"Did I what?"

"The law you invoked. The one, Glavik, said that the individual being challenged had the right to set the conditions."

"Yes, but..."

"You chose not to bring a retinue, Adrik," Falken cut his companion short. "You claimed that you did not want to appear outwardly threatening. Any fool would know better than to challenge a nominal leader in what could be a fight to the death." Falken remained even-toned as he spoke, shaking his head with disappointment. "You knew they would choose me to fight."

Adrik said nothing.

"When we first met, you seemed so genuine a friend to the others. It pains me to see just how much of a coward you are, in truth."

"I beg your pardon, sir," Adrik began to flush with anger. "I can understand that you are upset, but I had to make a tactical decision for the benefit of my subjects. I will not have you accuse me of cowardice!"

"Do not patronize me, Adrik." Falken remained calm and cold. "As a younger man, you were unable to face your eventual responsibilities as thane, so you avoided Citadel Moraben. As a widower, you were unable to face personal tragedy, so you left the Otharines altogether. You befriend a group of people who respect you, trust you, and when called home you were unable to face having to bid them farewell, choosing instead to leave them a cryptic note. The incident just now is only the latest in what I have observed as example after example of utter cowardice."

Again, the dwarf was silent, more so now for lack of having any manner of retort.

"I will not tell the others the truth of what happened here," Falken said finally. "Know that I am not doing this out of respect, though, as you have lost mine."

"Why, then?" Adrik asked finally.

"Because I believed that you were better than this, and seeing that image fade away hurt in such a way that I do not wish it upon any of the others."

The two riders were silent the remainder of the journey to Otharbund, Falken's eyes focusing intently on the path ahead, and Adrik wishing he were anywhere else in the world other than where he was, alone with his thoughts, more alone in some ways than he felt he had ever been.

Chapter 26

Daylen Cresthill sat in a large, comfortable chair in the personal office of Queen Merrian Arkalis, perched high within the Great Spire of Heavenguard. The headmaster tried his best to relax into the plush velvet, to try and mask his excited anticipation as Queen Merrian pored over the pages upon pages of parchment he had brought with him. The Queen's expression was one of stoicism as she passed from page to page of the headmaster's findings, causing Cresthill to become all the more anxious. After nearly half an hour's time, the Queen spoke, her eyes still transfixed on the pages.

"To look at them, one would think these the fevered scrawlings of a madman."

"In fairness, your Grace..."

"Daylen, please," Merrian interrupted absently, not meeting the headmaster's eyes, "we are alone. The formalities are unnecessary."

"Of course, Merrian," Cresthill corrected himself. "These are the notes of Falken Coldstone, of East Fellowdale."

"So they are indeed those of a madman," she noted, continuing to leaf through. "And yet, at the core... there is something to this..."

"It is extraordinary, isn't it?" Cresthill beamed. "The man's belongings were in an absolute state when I came upon them. Finding even the slightest bit of worthwhile information would take hours! As it stands, I have at least another three hundred pages I was able to find. The key, I think, is their organization into something more coherent." The headmaster stood, placing his hands on the far side of the Queen's desk, causing her to look up at him. "Merrian, I think I may have it, the secret of the origins of arcana, the truth behind it."

Queen Merrian smiled wryly back at the man. "That is as ambitious a statement as ever I have heard, Daylen. Though, if anyone has the drive to accomplish such a task, it is you."

"You flatter me, Merrian," Cresthill waved away the compliment. "Though you are correct in that I am determined to see this through. I've every intention of returning to the university first thing tomorrow, that I might use their resources in conjunction with this new information."

"The university?" the Queen stifled a delicate laugh. "Daylen, your modesty astounds me. You claim to be on the precipice of the greatest discovery of the modern age, and yet you are still content to preside over a mere school."

"And what would you have me do, Merrian?" the headmaster raised an incredulous eyebrow, a bit taken aback by the comment. "Sail the Windswept Sea and preside as Archmage over the barbarians of Majadrin?"

"Nothing so drastic," Merrian's expression sobered. "I trust... you were informed of Archmage Elbar?"

Cresthill's face mirrored his Queen's. "I did..." he nodded slowly. "It seemed so indignant a way for someone of his stature to die..."

"Well, he always did enjoy strolling the streets at night." Merrian reminisced, her tone somber. "I advised him against it so many times, you know. As much as I pride myself on the safety of Heavenguard, one cannot ever guarantee that some desperate madman won't take a knife to your back for a handful of coins." She shook her head distantly once more before looking back at Daylen Cresthill. "This does, however, leave the position of Archmage of Lohvast open, and I cannot think of someone whom I would feel more comfortable appointing to that position."

Cresthill looked back at the Queen, puzzled. "Merrian, I'm flattered, but how? You and I both know that I am not highborn, that I bear no claims or titles past that of Headmaster of Lohvast's arcane university."

"A simple matter," Merrian began, standing from the seat at her desk, "that I have already begun to remedy." She reached into a drawer at the desk's corner, withdrawing a piece of parchment. She walked to the opposite side of the desk and stood behind the headmaster's seat, slightly to one side, leaning over next to him as she lay the parchment down for him to read.

Her closeness did not cease, as she remained leaning next to him, the headmaster practically feeling her breath on him as he read the page. Cresthill's eyes widened as he skimmed the page, realizing the implications of the words written on it. "Merrian, this..." he stammered. "How are you...?"

"As you may know, Elbar had no family. Never married, had no siblings. The poor dear had told me often I felt like the only family he had, so I suppose he decided to leave his estate and title to me, neither of which I've much use for, but both of which I have to do with as I please."

"Will it not seem suspicious?" Cresthill asked finally. "The Archmage dies mysteriously, only for me to practically inherit his entire identity only weeks after the fact?"

Merrian placed a hand on the headmaster's shoulder, and he began to feel a sort of warmth, or calm wash over him as she spoke softly into his ear. "The people of Lohvast know who keeps them safe and warm, Daylen. A few words from their queen and the people of Lohvast will not so much as cast a sideways look at their new Archmage. Besides," she cooed, reaching for the quill sitting next to the parchment and placing it into the headmaster's hand, "once you discover the great secrets of arcana, there will not be a soul in all of the Four Kingdoms who would not kneel to you," she clasped her hand around his, motioning him to grip the quill. "To us."

Cresthill mulled over the idea in his mind as it began to sound increasingly promising. "I could have access to whatever knowledge I so wished," he mused, half to himself. "And, in truth, Archmage Cresthill does have a certain ring to it." Almost without knowing, Daylen Cresthill moved his arm to the bottom of the parchment, carefully signing his name, and in doing so changing everything he knew of his life and himself.

"Congratulations, Daylen," Queen Merrian smiled. "Or should I say 'Archmage Cresthill'?"

Chapter 27

I t took another full day of travel before Adrik and Falken arrived at Otharbund, during which time the pair said little to one another. Upon their arrival to the Morabendine camp, they were greeted warmly by Enna.

"How did it go?" she asked, running to them before they could even dismount their gryphons.

"Positively excelsior," Adrik smiled wearily, the statement lacking its typical enthusiasm. "I believe we have found allies in the other thaneships, and truly we have the good Professor to thank for our fortune."

"I was merely following your plan, Adrik," Falken replied, his own tone lacking its usual excitement as he slung some supplies from a saddlebag over his back. "Now if you will both excuse me, I'll go make camp." He walked off into the darkness without another word, causing Enna to give Adrik a quizzical look.

The dwarf shrugged. "The Professor is just a little road-weary, I'm sure. By Othar's beard, I am both a man of the road and of these mountains, and I am exhausted." He, too, gathered some supplies. "So, milady, if you do not mind..."

"Of course," Enna nodded and smiled as Adrik, too, walked away, though in an opposite direction from Falken. Enna pursed her lips into a frown as she stood alone. The two men were no doubt tired from their journey, but something seemed amiss with how they both were acting. She turned and walked toward where Falken had gone, hoping to find some better answers. The elf came upon the Professor soon thereafter, the various pieces of his tent strewn about the cavern floor as he huddled over a firepit, constructing a small pile of kindling, and cursing under his breath.

"Damned underground caverns with their damned lack of any real wood..." he muttered to himself as Enna approached. The elf could not help but let loose the slightest laugh at seeing the normally cheerful man become so frustrated by the act of building a campfire, an act she assumed an urbanite such as the professor was not particularly proficient with.

"Are you having some trouble, Falken?" she called out, causing the professor to start, and in doing so causing his meticulously crafted pyramid of kindling to collapse into a haphazard pile of sticks.

"Damn!" Falken cried out in exasperation before standing and turning to face Enna. "Ah, Enna..." he looked to the ground, weary and sheepish. "Forgive the outburst, my dear. I just... I was trying to... I've never..." he stammered.

The elf smiled and walked toward him. "I don't imagine you've done much camping in your life?" She stood next to him, and the pair turned to face the sad-looking bundle at the centre of the firepit.

"I know that propping the wood together at the top helps maintain the fire," Falken explained, "but there simply isn't any good, large logs or trees to be found here..."

As the professor spoke, Enna took her club from her belt and pointed it at the pile. Cutting the man off, she murmured a few Elvish words, releasing a bright orb of orange flame that streaked momentarily through the air before landing into the middle of the pit, setting the pile of wood ablaze.

"You're getting better at that," Falken noted, looking over at the elf.

Enna shrugged and smirked. "I still feel a little light-headed when I cast it. Not terribly, but enough that I need to wait some time before casting another spell." She looked over at the professor, her eyes meeting his. "Something went wrong when you and Adrik met the deep dwarves, didn't it?"

"Why would you assume that?" Falken asked back, quickly enough that it only further roused the elf's suspicion.

"Oh please, Falken, I'm not a child." she looked incredulously at the man. "You and he barely said two words to one another before you both ran off your separate ways. Now please, if there is anything wrong, anything that might be important to the matters at hand..."

"It's nothing," Falken tried to wave away Enna's concerns, his irritability beginning to show again. "A benign little argument we had before we arrived back here. We'll both be over it after we get some rest."

"An argument?" Enna laughed. "That's funny, Adrik's the last person I would expect to argue with anyone."

"Well, perhaps you don't know him as well as you might think," Falken's response was so curt it took Enna aback.

"What's that supposed to mean?" The elf's irritability was now starting to show, as well.

"Nothing," the professor replied dismissively. "Now, I am sorry Enna, but if you don't mind I would like to retire."

Enna glared at the professor. "Fine, I'll go find Adrik. Perhaps he'll tell me what you refuse to."

Before Falken could respond, the sound of some manner of ruckus could be heard from the other side of the camp. Enna looked back at the professor concernedly, who then nodded in silent agreement, collected his wand, and began to run with his fellow arcanist toward the sound of shouting dwarves.

The two arrived at a barracks tent on the outermost edge of the Morabendine camp to find the source of the noise. A pair of dwarves held a third, clothed in colours that were distinctly not those of Morabendar. The captive thrashed and struggled as a crowd formed about the scene, several of them holding many of the others at arm's length from the captive. The crowd calmed somewhat as Merida Mettlehelm stormed through the mob to face the dwarf being held at bay. She said something to the captive in Dwarfish, the captive responding in kind in what seemed to Enna an even tone.

"What are they saying?" Enna whispered to Falken, who was watching the meeting intently.

"He's an Ulbar scout, from what I can tell." The Professor's eyes did not leave the interrogation. "He claims the first wave of Ulbar forces are only a day's travel away from Otharbund, that they are aware of Morabendar's plans, and can easily outnumber and overwhelm us..."

"It could be a bluff," Enna offered. "For all we know he may have just stumbled across the camp."

"Even if he had, we already know Morabendar is outnumbered, there's no reason for him to lie about the rest of it..."

With a final shouted command by Merida, the two dwarves holding the Ulbar scout pulled him away into the camp as the commander stormed off in the other direction, no doubt to relay her findings to Adrik. Enna and Falken followed pensively, their curiosity and concern tempered by the fact that Merida would likely only be annoyed by their presence. As she arrived at the large tent that had been set up as a war room, Enna and Falken stayed outside and at a distance. The Professor strained to hear the discussion between thane and commander over the din of the rest of the camp as Enna watched his face intently, trying to glean some insight from his reactions. After a few moments, Falken needed to struggle no longer, as full-volume shouting began to erupt from both parties inside the tent. Enna saw the Professor's eyes go wide with surprise upon hearing something Adrik had said.

"What?" Enna asked, clutching at his sleeve worriedly. "What is it?"

Before Falken could answer, the two dwarves came bursting out of the tent, Adrik marching out ahead as Merida followed closely behind, still shouting at him. Adrik seemingly ignored his sister's every word as he carried on, determination evident in his every step, until she finally turned him around to face her, speaking so low that Falken could not hear. Adrik deflated visibly as his sister spoke, finally nodding his head slowly before turning back around and continuing, his stride now carrying less grandeur. The pair made their way back to the barracks tent, where the crowd out front had not yet dissipated. The soldiers, spotting Adrik, quickly bowed and moved to attention, only to have him wave away the formalities and usher a command to one of them, who quickly saluted the thane and darted inside the tent, shouting something to all those within.

Falken and Enna watched as Adrik gave the same command to a few others, each of them running off in different directions. Soon enough, the whole of the Morabendine camp was present, roughly five hundred in all, most of which were soldiers. All stood in wait, looking up at Adrik, who had climbed atop a small pile of supply crates. Merdia simply stood and looked up surreptitiously at her brother. Once the thane seemed satisfied that no one was absent, he began to speak with confidence and authority. Falken, needing no provocation from Enna, began to translate to her what was being said.

"Friends, we have come upon the news this eve that Ulbar forces are not but a day's travel from Otharbund. Whether or not they are aware of our own arrival is uncertain, but what is certain is that they mean to march on Morabendar, on our home. We must prevent this at all costs." Adrik paused only briefly, his audience remaining silent as he continued. "Lady Merida has set in place a plan for an ambush on the Ulbar forces as they pass into Otharbund, on which I am confident she has given you all thorough instruction. I implore each and every one of you to follow these instructions to the letter, in the hopes that we may hold Ulbaryn at bay long enough that we might bide our time until forces from Arvadem and Bakraam can come to our aid. I have formed a pact with our neighbours to the south, and have..." The dwarf paused and swallowed hard. He looked down at Merida a moment, her eyes widening in frustration and her mouth about to open to say something before he cut her off by continuing.

"Friends... when I returned to Morabendar some weeks ago, I had not seen but the northernmost reaches of our beloved Otharines for decades. In truth, I have spent more of my life outside the Thaneship unto which I have claim than inside it. I did not wish to share the responsibilities of my father, and his father before him. By Othar's beard, when I did return I hid myself away in the recesses of Citadel Moraben, unable to face the people for whom I am now accountable. Looking at the lot of you, all at the ready to lay down your lives, I cannot help but ask myself 'why?' Surely you've no reason to fight in the name of one who did not even have the dignity to spend but a fortnight among his people before begrudgingly asking their fealty. I am not asking you to fight for that person, that coward." Falken seemed to stumble somewhat as he translated the final part.

"If I am to be your thane," Adrik continued, "then I will do so with pride and honour. I will not simply sit idly in the background, sending you to the front lines to fight, perchance to die in my name. No, friends, when the Ulbar army descends upon us, I shall be in those front lines, mace in hand, shoulder-to-shoulder with all of you, come good or ill." There came a smattering of applause amid the soldiers. "And when the battle is won, and we drive back this threat, I swear upon the Lord and Scions alike, I will not cower in Citadel Moraben, wallowing in hereditary gains as others decide your fates. I swear to return to Morabendar among you, my people, and to ensure that I am one who is truly deserving of my title, and of my people..."

The whole of the camp now erupted in a chorus of uproarious applause, and before her eyes Enna saw not Adrik the dwarven merchant whom she had befriended in Hallowspire what seemed like a lifetime ago, but Adrik Thornmallet, Thane of

Morabendar, a leader and doubtless soon to be victor in the battle to come.

Chapter 28

"Hold a moment," Erasmus Stonehand called to his partner as he limped awkwardly several feet behind, squinting to look at the map in his hands under the now dimmed runelamps. "I think we might be lost."

"We are lost," O'doc said irritably. "We've been wandering for the last two days, and by that map we ought to have reached at least one or two of the outlying Ulbar towns. For Sheandre's sake, we've not even passed by another caravan of soldiers!"

"Could be that we've gone around the outskirts of the Thaneship," Erasmus offered as he sat on a large rock and began to massage his sore leg. "Gods, I didn't expect all this walking to wear on me so much."

"Well, you didn't see what you looked like before Brother Morgran knitted you back together," O'doc murmured. "And what do you mean 'gone around'? Erasmus, we're not back in the kingdoms, there aren't wide expanses of land. All these tunnels were built with purpose. There's no way to 'go around.'"

"Isn't there?" Erasmus looked at the halfling calmly. "This map is Morabendine."

"What does that matter?" O'doc asked. "It was one of the most recent maps in Lady Merida's possession."

"It's perfectly reasonable to assume that Ulbaryn could have tunnels that whoever drew this map wasn't aware of."

"How, Erasmus?" O'doc prodded, his whole body a picture of fatigue and irritability. "Please explain to me how one manages to construct vast expanses of underground tunnels without anyone else noticing, and then proceeds to hide those tunnels?"

Erasmus rolled his eyes and shrugged. "I don't know. All I'm saying is that there has to be some reason behind..." he stopped mid-sentence, cocking his head to one side and raising a hand to shush O'doc. "I hear footsteps," he said in a low whisper. "Hide, now."

The pair scrambled into the shadows, finding cover in a nearby outcropping of stalagmites. O'doc crouched low and drew his daggers, while Erasmus, feeling the pain surge through his leg with the sudden movement, sat with his back against one of the taller spires of stone, listening intently in the direction of the footsteps.

"Just one," the half-elf whispered. "Heavy-footed, no doubt a dwarf."

"I see him," the halfling whispered back, grinning as he spotted a lone dwarf round the bend down the tunnel, wearing no weapons but a small hand axe. "I think we have a way out." He looked to

Erasmus, and then to the supplies that lay next to him. The bard caught O'doc's eye once more and gave a knowing wink, reaching for the leather case that held his cherished mandolin as O'doc drew two pieces of soft candle wax from a pouch in his belt and began to place them in either ear. The halfling turned his attention back to the dwarf, who stopped almost instantly in his tracks as soon as the soft strumming of Erasmus Stonehand began to fill the air, echoing off the tunnel's stone walls. The dwarf drew his hand axe and looked about the tunnel intently, as though he were trying to pinpoint where the impromptu music was originating. Before the half-elf had even begun to sing his enchanted words, however, O'doc saw the dwarf's head turn sharply toward the stalagmites in which the pair hid. The dwarf's body followed suit, proceeding then to walk tentatively toward the hiding place.

O'doc looked over at Erasmus, who was in the midst of weaving his charm, then back at the gradually encroaching dwarf. The halfling had seen his partner cast this particular charm numerous times, and it was evident to him that the dwarf would no doubt come upon the two before it was complete. As the Elvish lyrics of the bard's ballad began to echo through the tunnel in the bard's raspy tenor, O'doc took a deep breath and leaped out from his hiding place directly at the dwarf.

The dwarf hurled his hand axe almost reflexively at O'doc, but the suddenness of the halfling's appearance visibly startled him, causing the axe to sail wide of its target, landing with an ineffectual clatter in the shadows. O'doc was upon the dwarf an instant later, bearing the butts of his daggers rather than the blades. The dwarf lashed out with his thick arms, trying to grapple his assailant, but the small, spry halfling tumbled out to the way. He saw a number of openings in the dwarf's defenses, whereby he could incapacitate his stout opponent with a single blow, but withheld, reminding himself that he and Erasmus needed this dwarf to have his wits about him if he was to be of any use.

Caught up in his own thoughts, and already at the disadvantage of being unable to hear what was going on around him, O'doc reeled as he felt the heel of the dwarf's boot connect with his back, drawing the air from his lungs and causing him to sprawl onto the cold ground in front of him. The dwarf knelt down on the halfling now, his thick shin like a tree trunk that pinned down all of O'doc's upper body while his hands held the sell-sword's arms easily. O'doc wriggled and wrestled, trying to escape the restraining hold, but the dwarf's sheer size and strength outmatched any attempts.

Suddenly, O'doc felt the dwarf's grip soften slightly, though his full weight still rested on the halfling's back. The slack was enough, however, for O'doc to wrest his hands free, the dwarf's arms falling slack as he did so. Removing the plugs from his ears, O'doc could hear no music, and smiled in relief, knowing Erasmus' spell must have taken effect. He heard the half-elf walk over to the two, his footfalls still indicating a slight limp.

"Can you understand the northern tongue?" the bard's raspy voice spoke.

"Aye," the dwarf replied.

"Good. Release the halfling." The dwarf did so, and O'doc rolled over onto his back, gasping and choking as he sucked in gulps of the dry tunnel air.

"Who are you?" Erasmus asked the dwarf.

"Valak Ryngrym." the dwarf replied impassively.

"And where are we right now, Valak Ryngrym?"

"This tunnelway has not yet been named. It is the private passageway by which Thane Zanak attends his meetings with Him."

"...Him?" Erasmus raised an eyebrow.

Valak Ryngrym nodded, unblinking. "The one who has given Thane Zanak control of the stone."

Erasmus looked over to O'doc, who was only able to muster a concerned look and a shrug. "You will take us to where Thane Zanak attends these meetings."

The dwarf nodded and began to lead the sell-swords further into the passage from whence he had come. After a time they came upon a nondescript doorway in the stone, a strange glyph that was neither elven nor dwarven carved into the stone above it. The dwarf stood at the side of the doorway and motioned at it.

"What is beyond this doorway?" Erasmus asked.

"Stairs spiral downward," the dwarf answered plainly. "Beyond that, I do not know. All but Thane Zanak are forbidden from entering."

"I bid you enter with us," Erasmus said.

The dwarf did not hesitate, walking between O'doc and Erasmus as they descended the staircase. There were no runelamps, and so O'doc lit a candle as they descended. At the bottom of the stairs, the dim glow of the halfling's candle revealed something that gave him pause. A plain wooden door bearing the same glyph as was above the doorway from which the trio had entered. He looked back at Erasmus. "Have you seen a single door made of wood in our entire time down here?"

"Not one." Erasmus shook his head gravely. "See what's inside."

Swallowing nervously, O'doc pulled at the door's handle, and entered. The room was pitch black, but smelled distinctly of musty old books. The creaking of the doors hinges echoed in such a way as to give the halfling some idea of the room's size. It was tall, and deep, almost impossibly so. "Erasmus," he called back to the bard, a sickly feeling of deja vu forming in the pit of his stomach. "Could you have our new friend here describe what he might see in here?"

"Can you see well enough without light?" Erasmus asked the dwarf.

"As well as a northerner might see by runelamp."

"Good. Step through that doorway and tell me what you see."

The dwarf nodded and entered the room, looking about it a moment before answering. "It is a large room, like a library. There are tall bookshelves on either side of the room, as well as tables made of wood. There is a large laneway down the middle."

O'doc's eyes widened and his stomach sank as the dwarf described a room that sounded far too much like the library beneath Falken's manor. He looked up at Erasmus, and could see that similar thoughts were going through the half-elf's mind as well.

"What is at the other end of the room?" Erasmus asked, though he and O'doc both knew the answer before it was given.

"A door made of wood."

Both sell-swords knew also what would be past that door. Both remembered the immense power that pulsed through that small room, with its strange glowing orbs and stone dias. Neither had any desire to trifle with that power right now. The trio left the strange place quickly, and when they were out Erasmus gave O'doc a knowing look. "I think our friend the professor has some explaining to do."

O'doc nodded reluctantly. His family had known Falken for years, and while he was admittedly a bit odd, O'doc knew there wasn't a malicious bone in his body. At least, it was what he was telling himself right now. He knew in either case, though, that he and Erasmus needed to get back to Otharbund as quick as possible.

Erasmus, evidently sharing the halfling's sentiment, withdrew the map and showed it to the dwarf. "Do you know the route the Ulbar army is taking to Otharbund?"

The dwarf nodded, and traced the path along the map with his finger.

"From where we are, what path might we take to avoid the army?" Erasmus fumbled through his pack a moment, finding a candle of deep red and handing it to the dwarf. "Draw it."

The dwarf obliged, mapping out their current position, just northeast of the Ulbar capital, and drawing a winding line through a series of tunnels that eventually ended at a northern entrance into Otharbund.

"How long will this take to travel?"

"Two days or more by foot."

"Do you have any steeds?"

The dwarf nodded. "A supply cart driven by two gryphons."

"Fetch it for us, quickly," Erasmus said. "When we leave, you are to return to your home and sleep, remembering nothing of what you saw and heard today." The dwarf nodded, and ran with haste further down the tunnel, returning shortly thereafter with the cart and gryphons. The sell-swords clamboured into it, Erasmus taking the reigns of the gryphons. "Off now, to home, to rest," he said, looking down at the dwarf. "You have our thanks, Valak Ryngrym."

The dwarf simply nodded and began to walk away as Erasmus tried to bring the gryphons to as quick a pace as possible. As they made their way through the tunnels, O'doc prayed silently to Sheandre, both in the hopes that they would reach Otharbund in time to help their friends, and that in doing so, it would not mean having to save them from one in their midst.

Chapter 29

The Battle of Otharbund began swiftly and abruptly, with the Morabendine forces successfully ambushing the first of several Ulbar military caravans. As promised, Adrik remained on the front lines, albeit with a personal retinue of Merida's choosing, proudly wielding the bronze mace he acquired from what seemed like another lifetime ago as he felled soldiers from the enemy thaneship. By the end of the first day of the battle, both sides suffered losses, but the ambush seemed to have worked in Morabendar's favour, and its thane felt a glimmer of hope that perhaps the battle would be a swift affair. By the third consecutive day, however, with no sign of the deep dwarves, and far more reinforcements arriving from Ulbaryn than Morabendar, the dwarf began to feel his body tire. He was at least twice the age of most of the soldiers he had been standing, and the relentlessness of the fighting was more than Adrik had been used to since he was their age, if not in his entire life. As such, it was with no small amount of relief that he recieved the news from a page that Commander Mettlehelm had ordered him to stand down for the evening and report to her quarters at their camp.

Adrik was exhausted and weary as he made his way to Merida's quarters, a large tent dyed the grey and gold of Morabendar, serving both as living quarters for she and Morgran, and as a tactical centre, with a large table with sprawling maps and diagrams serving as the centrepoint of the tent's interior. Adrik was saluted by the guards at the tent's entrance, returning the gesture halfheartedly. As he walked into the tent, Adrik's face brightened suddenly as it came upon Erasmus and O'doc, both standing at the war table speaking with Merida.

"Our scouts have returned to the fray!" he said mirthfully as he approached, smiling broadly and clapping each of them on the shoulder as they turned to face him. "What news from amid the Ulbar ranks?"

"None that would be terribly beneficial to the battle, I'm afraid," O'doc said grimly.

"Well, that all depends on what the professor has to say," Erasmus added with a mirthless chuckle.

"What do you mean?" Adrik asked, unsure of how to take the half-elf's comment.

"He means," O'doc was quick to answer, "that we found something odd along the northern reaches of Ulbar, similar to something we saw at Falken's manor."

"Will you quit side-stepping this?" Erasmus cut in. "Since when did you of all people become so damned trusting?"

"Falken and my aunt have been close friends for years," O'doc protested. "If there were anything about him that seemed off, she'd not have sent us his way."

"I'm sorry," a man's voice came from the entrance to the tent. In the heat of the sell-swords' argument, no one had noticed Enna and Falken enter, led by the same young page who had summoned Adrik. Falken approached the centre of the tent as he spoke. "Erasmus, I had thought we had gotten past whatever pettiness that was hanging about us some time ago."

"I've got much more than 'mere pettiness' to discuss with you." Erasmus glared at the professor. "That... place... library... whatever it is below your home... I want to know what it is and where it came from, and gods help me you'd best tell me everything you know."

Falken looked at Erasmus with a face of utter confusion. "Why is that even relevant right now?"

"Answer the question now, openly and in truth," Erasmus spoke slow and pointedly, "or I will use what means I have to force the truth from you."

"Erasmus!" Enna stormed over to the bard. "What is the matter with you? We've been in the mountains for a month, and now this is a problem?"

"That place was always a problem for me," Erasmus answered, his eyes remaining fixed on Falken, "but when O'doc and I found an exact replica of it in a secret tunnel-way north of Ulbaryn, I think it became a problem for everyone."

"A what?" Falken's eyes widened. "How could that be?"

"Don't play coy, Professor," Erasmus rolled his eyes. "The act's getting tired."

"It's not an act, you impulsive twit," Falken shook his hand dismissively at the half-elf, his eyes now far away and ponderous. "I had always thought something was extraordinary about that place..."

"Falken," O'doc stepped forward and grabbed the arcanist by the forearm, bringing his attention back to the tent. All eyes therein had begun to take on a suspicious look, save O'doc's. "You're not doing yourself any favours right now... please..."

Falken sighed and nodded. "I understand that this may look more than a little unseemly, but truly, all I know of that place is what I told you back in East Fellowdale."

"The dwarf who led us there told us that Thane Zanak used it as a place to speak with 'Him'," O'doc mentioned. "Do you have any idea what that might mean?"

Adrik and Merida looked more intently on the professor now, who only shook his head and shrugged. "I haven't the faintest clue..."

"I don't believe you," Erasmus said shortly.

"Then bind me to a chair and cast a truth charm on me!" Falken shot back in exasperation.

"I had planned to," Erasmus retorted, though the sound of alarm bells throughout the camp kept the heated conversation from escalating any further. The group began to exit the tent, as Erasmus stared at the professor once more. "We are not finished here," he stated simply before he left.

Out in the front of Merida's tent, the group was met by one of the commander's senior captains. "Milady, Lord," she spoke in Dwarfish, saluting Merida and Adrik.

"If you've news on the battle, Captain, speak in the northern tongue," Merida returned the salute, but spoke in common. "All those present are involved, and I'll not have you waste time repeating yourself."

The captain gave a subtle look of quiet surprise, but nodded and continued as directed. "Another wave of Ulbar forces have arrived at the front."

"What manner of forces?" Merida asked. "Infantry? Cavalry?"

"Infantry, milady." the captain hesitated. "That is to say, an infantry of some sort..."

"Speak plainly, Captain!"

The captain nodded once more. "Dwarven infantry mostly, milady, but something else as well... creatures that look like dwarves, but made of stone, and moving of their own accord."

Merida's lips formed a tight line. "I see. Any sign of reinforcements from Arvadem and Barkaan?"

"None yet, milady."

Merida cursed under her breath. "Scour the armaments for whatever hammers, maces, and any other blunt weapons you can find, and equip the troops accordingly." The captain nodded, and was off. Merida and turned to look at Falken and Enna.

"My troops won't stand a fighting chance against those things for very long. Morgran may be able to concoct something with our runemages, but that will take time. Both of you head to the gryphon riders, drop whatever fae witchery you can from above." Both arcanists nodded and made for the aviary pens.

"Stonehand," the dwarf turned now to Erasmus. "You're still weak, no good to me in open combat," she looked him up and down, "but it seems you've some skill in persuasion. See what you can do out there to persuade the enemy to make some mistakes." Erasmus smirked and bowed. "Overhill," she added, looking to the halfling "keep close to him, and make sure neither of you get killed."

"Milady," O'doc saluted the dwarf before he and Erasmus made off as well.

Merida turned now to Adrik and spoke to him in Dwarfish, her tone and eyes somewhat softened. "You know what I'll say, and I know you'll just ignore it, so I'll say this instead: be careful, brother." She looked him in his violet eyes. "You've become so much greater a man than I could have dreamed. Father would be proud."

Adrik took one of his sister's gauntlet-clad hands in both of his, and smiled. "We could use all the assistance we can muster out there. What say we march on those abominations shoulder-to-shoulder, for Clan Thornmallet?"

A small smirk began to form at the corner of Merida Mettlehelm's mouth, as a resolute look came across her face. "For Clan Thornmallet," she nodded.

The floor of the battlefield had rumbled for the past two days under the feet of the two dwarven armies so frequently that it no longer seemed to phase Adrik. The rumble he felt as he stepped onto the front now, however, gave the dwarf pause. This was not only due to the fact that the vibrations were now visibly shaking him, but more so because of the sight he witnessed before him. During the first few days of battle, Adrik had become accustomed to seeing a few score Ulbar soldiers march into the 'fore. Now, he witnessed at least double that many forces marching forward, dwarves mostly, but others in their midst, all a dull gray, and all roughly the same size and shape of a dwarf. They held no weapons, as they had no fists, nor did they have any other distinct features past their bodies and limbs. Adrik clenched at his mace in anticipation, looking over to his sister, who did the same with her maul.

"If you've a bludgeoning weapon and a clear hit, attack the stone soldiers." Merida called out to the infantry behind her. "Other than that, focus on the fleshy ones, and keep your heads up for any fire raining from above."

Behind Adrik and Merida there was a chorus of assent. Merida raised her maul and let out a great battle cry, she and Adrik leading the charge onto the battlefield. The Ulbar forces began to charge in kind,

Adrik noted that the stone creatures lumbered behind the dwarves at a much slower pace. It was not long before the forces crashed headlong into one another, Adrik stared intently into the eyes of the first soldier he rushed as he rammed his mace directly into the enemy dwarf's breastplate, quickly pushing the foe aside as they gulped for air and crumpled to the ground. Two more were upon the thane almost instantly, one of whom he quickly felled as he swung the mace head into the soldier's leg, audibly snapping the thighbone as the soldier wailed in pain. The second menaced a large axe over Adrik's head, but was quickly dispatched by Merida, whose maul's practiced upward swing made contact with the assailant's chin, sending him floating through the air for a moment before landing in a heap next to her.

From up above, Adrik spotted several small flickers of light that quickly descended onto the battlefield; they were spears tipped with fire that glowed brightly as they crashed down. Any of the flaming projectiles that did not find purchase in a foe would at least provide enough of a distraction away from the blades of the charging Morabendine soldiers. Adrik himself used the distractions to forge a path deeper into the battlefield, bobbing through or otherwise striking down those in his path, until he was nearly through to the other side of the thick of the fighting. He was stopped by a hand on his shoulder, and spun about-face to see Merida.

"What are you doing?" she cried. "You're not five strides away from those creatures!"

Adrik nodded. "I've got a clear hit. What ho!" And with that, the dwarf turned back around, moving in a full charge toward the approaching stone beings.

"I can barely see anything up here!" Falken cried out over the sound of the gryphons' wings.

"Never mind with seeing!" the cavalrymaid with whom he was riding cried back. "Just keep lighting the tips of those spears and let me worry about where they fly."

Falken nodded, setting the tip of another spear ablaze with arcane fire and handing it off to the rider. Across the way, he spotted Enna, trying her best to enchant the arrows her rider was hailing down on the battlefield. "How goes it?" he called out to her.

Enna looked up after handing an arrow to the rider, her face grim. "They're outnumbered down there," she called back. "I don't know how long they can hold out." She looked back down at the arrows, only to have her eyes widen. "Oh gods, Adrik!"

"What happened?" Falken called, lighting another spear ablaze.

"He's running toward those creatures!" She tapped the rider on the arm. "You have to take me down there!"

"You'll be killed, surely!" he answered back gruffly. "And I have my orders from Lady Merida."

"Your thane will be killed if you let him charge into those stone soldiers alone!" she protested.

The dwarf said nothing a moment, loosed an arrow onto the field, and said finally, "I'll fly you overhead of those things, let you cast some spells overhead, but I'll not let you touch the ground."

The gryphon carrying Enna dipped and swooped away, and Falken looked to his own rider. "Where are they going?"

"Well, I didn't discuss it with them, but it looks like they're headed toward the rear lines of the Ulbar forces, those stone soldiers."

Falken's eyes widened. "Stone soldiers?! We have to follow them!"

The cavalrymaid shrugged. "Your choice, I'm just your eyes up here." In an instant their own gryphon changed course, swooping now behind Enna's.

As much as it would have been to Lady Merida's consternation, O'doc noted as he firmly planted a dagger into the exposed rib of an Ulbar assailant, he and Erasmus had never been particularly good at keeping themselves out of trouble. Even along the outskirts of the battlefield, the pair just happened to stumble upon a number of Ulbar soldiers who had broken rank to relieve themselves, and who were, much to the halfling's surprise and chagrin, quicker at readying themselves for a fight than he expected.

Typically, six to two would work in the sell-swords' favour, doubly so when the six were wearing cumbersome plate armor, but the dwarves had the advantage in the dim cavern, and the half-elf was slower on his feet than he had been, and was struggling to fend off two at the same time after felling one with his short-sword. O'doc did what he could, but was dancing and parrying amid two combatants of his own, just narrowly missing a number of axe and sword swings as he searched for openings in the dwarves' armour. Suddenly, all the present combatants ceased their fighting, as a strange tapping sound began to swell around them. In an instant, a number of dwarves, pale-skinned with small dark eyes and large pronounced ears, began to march toward the group, stopping suddenly, but all tapping tall staves to the ground several more times before ceasing.

One of the strange pale dwarves said something in a strange dialect that O'doc, even having spent a month in the Otharines, did not recognize. The dwarf seemed to look at no one in particular as he spoke, but one of the Ulbar dwarves answered, something to the effect of serving Thane Zanak. The pale dwarf nodded, and motioned forward, speaking what sounded to O'doc like some kind of order. Instantly, half the group of strange dwarves were upon the Ulbar soldiers, quickly and efficiently overwhelming and defeating them, as

Erasmus and O'doc stood agog at the scene that unfolded.

The dwarf who evidently commanded the others strode over to the sell-swords, asking the same question to them as he had the Ulbar dwarves. O'doc hesitated a moment before slowly, tentatively replying, "...Thane Adrik? Morabendar?"

The pale dwarf nodded, and called out to the others with him. Before Either O'doc or Erasmus could make sense of what had just happened, they found themselves marching in time with the strange band. "These are our allies, I assume?" Erasmus leaned over and whispered to O'doc mid-march.

"I hope so," the halfling shrugged, "or I gather we're in for far worse trouble that six soldiers in the middle of a piss..."

Chapter 30

E nna could see the battle shifting quickly as they gryphon soared tens of feet overhead. It looked as though, by her estimation, the fabled deep dwarf allies Adrik and Falken had secured had finally arrived, and were quickly spreading into the 'fore. She relaxed some as she saw others begin to flank the area past the main fight, where the strange stone creatures continued to march toward Adrik, and only perhaps another five or six Morabendine soldiers. The elf pointed her club carefully and called out an incantation, dropping several fireballs into the middle of the creatures, all of which simply landed on one of the stone bodies and ineffectually dissipated. The uselessness of her spell caused that relaxation to wane, doubly so as she looked on to see two of the Morabendine soldiers challenge a creature each in open combat, each meeting swift defeat as large stone fists cast them aside with the ease of a child throwing a ragdoll.

"You need to get me down there!" she cried to the cavalryman controlling the gryphon.

"Are you mad?" he exclaimed."I'll not send you to your death so quickly, northerner."

Enna looked at the scene below as a wave of complete helplessness washed over her. Even with the deep dwarf support, it was taking at least four dwarves to overwhelm a single construct. There had to be something she could do. Suddenly, along one flank, she spotted the remains of one construct that had been destroyed by a number of dwarves, now a large pile of rubble. The size of the stone chunks left in the construct's wake gave her an idea.

"Swoop down low," she told the cavalryman, pointing to the remains. "Have your gryphon snatch the largest chunks in its talons, and drop them on the creatures!"

"A fine plan, lady!" the dwarf responded, and proceeded to do as he was bade. The gryphon cawed ferociously as it dipped, snatching several pieces of rock, and proceeded to drop them into the midst of the constructs. Only the largest of the stone pieces was effective, but it was one less construct, nonetheless.

Not far behind Enna, Falken continued to squint down into the murky darkness of the battlefield.

"You couldn't see before," the professor's cavalrymaid partner chided him. "What makes you think you'll see now?"

"Things... sound different now." Falken answered. "What's going on?"

"Reinforcements have arrived," the dwarf answered. "Helping against the Ulbar forces, but don't seem to be much good against those stone beasts..." She paused a moment, before adding "...now that's an idea!"

"What?" Falken asked. "What's an idea?"

"Horym couldn't have been that clever," the dwarf replied, half to herself. "I think that fae ladyfriend of yours may have helped us turn the tides on this." Without another word the cavalrymaid dipped her gryphon into a dive, so fast that Falken had to clasp onto her.

Enna looked about the see Falken's gryphon diving down, hopefully following her lead. Below, a handful more of the Morabendine soldiers had broken through to aid against the constructs, most of whom did their best to keep Adrik out of the fray, or in the very least give aid to the thane against the stone creatures he had attempted to fight. He was quickly tiring and becoming slow, Enna noticed, and his mace swings were becoming sluggish. He needed more help, and there were only so many soldiers available to aid him.

"Keep dropping those stones," she told the cavalryman as the gryphon came down low again. "If anything happens, be sure to tell Lady Merida that this was my doing."

Before the dwarf could respond, Enna dropped off the gryphon's side, muttering the words to a levitation spell Falken had taught her to soften her fall. The elf sped over to aid Adrik, watching in horror as four of the constructs encroached on the dwarf, each swing of his mace having less effect than the last, until the four constructs were upon him, swallowing him up in their midst.

"Adrik!" Enna cried, tears of rage and sorrow combining as her mind began to race. Adrik had shown Enna, and all those around him, nothing but kindness and selflessness. The dwarf did not deserve this fate, to be crushed by sorcerous abominations in a war he wished to not be a part of. The elf's thoughts began to turn into seething rage, until she began to move as though she were under some kind of charm. The tears in her eyes gave way to a quiet, deathly calm, and she raised her club to the mob of constructs at her fallen friend.

The gem embedded in the club's head glowed a ferocious, intense emerald hue, so bright that many in the nearby area had to shield their eyes. The elf spoke the words of a spell, and in an instant had pulled the constructs from Adrik, who now lay crumpled on the stone ground. Enna's eyes did not linger on her fallen friend. She was sure he was gone, and her thoughts were filled now solely with inflicting pain in kind, pain on those responsible for Adrik, and for Erasmus, and for this whole damnable war.

The constructs hung suspended in the air, glowing a similar emerald hue as they were guided by the elf's implement. In a swift motion, she brought the stone forms down to bear on the few constructs felt around her, striking down hard as though she were controlling a large, ethereal hammer, slamming the controlled constructs down repeatedly, until all that was left of their comrades was rubble.

All fighting had at this point halted, as all stood in awe of the arcane display, yet Enna paid the cease in combat no mind. Her body was ablaze with arcane power, and her mind was rife with vengeful desire. She quickly turned the suspended constructs on a number of Ulbar soldiers, who frantically scrambled in an attempt to avoid their doom. Three of the squad were unfortunate enough to be slower on their feet than the rest, and the cracking and screams of them being crushed under the weight of their own forces were drowned out by the horrified cries of the remainder of the Ulbar forces retreating.

In a final burst of arcane energy, Enna slammed the four constructs under her control into one another, until they, too, were reduced to rubble. Then, as suddenly as it came, all the energy Enna Summerlark possessed was stricken from her. She fell to her knees, in the middle of a battlefield that had been littered by bodies, some friends, some foes, and some whom Enna slew by her own hands. The elf, overwhelmed by the whole of it all, collapsed into thick, choking sobs on the cold stone floor. She saw nothing of what unfolded after, not wanting to open her eyes and make it all real once more. Cries of battle surged up once more, but further off now. Ulbar was being pushed back, she hoped. She heard the cries of Merida Mettlehelm, calling for help to aid the fallen thane. Finally, she felt a reassuring hand on her shoulder, and heard a voice speak to her softly.

"Come now, my dear, it's all over," came the voice of Falken Coldstone. Enna willed herself to open her eyes, and through her tears she saw the Professor extending his hand to her. She took it and only barely managed to stand. Looking across the way, she saw Erasmus and O'doc helping with Adrik, the old dwarf's body more bloodied and contorted than even Erasmus' had been. She looked away from the scene swiftly, and began to walk back to camp, though the entire trip back was no more than a blur in which the only thing that felt real was Falken's reassuring voice, telling her that everything would be all right.

Several long hours passed, during which time Enna did not move from where she sat outside the tent where Adrik had been treated by Brother Morgran, among a number of other clerics. The fact that the dwarf had survived the attack was a wonder in and of itself, but the question of whether or not he would make it through the next few nights was on the lips of all at the camp. The nights came and went, and though Adrik did not worsen, he did not wake, and Enna did not move. Erasmus came to sit with the elf on her third night of waiting, telling her everything that he and O'doc had discovered on their expedition.

"So there will be war back home, too?" Enna said quietly, then let out a mirthless laugh. "Did the whole world decide to go to the hells at once?" She stared out into the camp for a while. "Deep down, there was a part of me that enjoyed it, seeing them die," she said, her eyes still far away.

Erasmus said nothing, instead resting a sympathetic hand on her shoulder. "For what it's worth," he said after a time, "I'm going to lay off Falken."

"So you admit you were being paranoid?" Enna let the smallest hint of a smirk form at one side of her mouth.

"I didn't say that," the half-elf retorted. "I still think there has to be some connection between those two identical libraries," he started, "but I saw the way he helped you out there the other day. Whatever connection he has to what O'doc and I found, and I still believe there is one, it's clear he means you no harm. I can deal with that."

Before Enna could respond, she heard loud coughing from inside Adrik's tent. Her eyes went wide, and she looked over at Erasmus. "Go find Brother Morgran, I'll gather the others." With a short nod from the bard, both were on their feet, reconvening a short time later with O'doc, Falken, and the Mettlehelms. They all looked worriedly at one another before pulling back the folds of the tent to find Adrik Thornmallet, sitting upright on the cot in which he'd lain for the past three nights. His face was still badly bruised, bearing a forlorn look as he examined what remained of his left arm, a bandaged stump that ended just above where his elbow had once been. The dwarf looked up at his visitors, and the frown gave way to a weary smile. "This will, no doubt, merit some time for adjustment."

Merida was the first to embrace her brother, pulling him tightly into a hug. "If you ever do anything that stupid again," she said, her voice quivering, "I'll string you up for all of Deltharduin to see, you hear me?"

"Left in your husband's capable hands," Adrik retorted with a chuckle. "I am not sure I would have anything left by which you could string me." He looked at his sister with serious eyes now. "What of Ulbaryn?"

"Retreated," Merida replied. "Three days now since we've had any sign of them."

Adrik nodded. "Would that the news eased my nerves. No war was ever won in a day."

"I'm sure Lohvast's army of warmages plan on proving that old adage wrong," O'doc said grimly.

Adrik gave the halfling a puzzling look. "Troubling news from the north?"

"From an Ulbar soldier, actually," O'doc replied. "Apparently Queen Merrian had asked Zanak for military aid, but he declined."

"You must return north with haste, then!" Adrik said, straightening himself.

"Adrik we're not just going to abandon..." Enna began to protest, but stopped. "Wait... 'you'?"

Adrik nodded assuredly. "Indeed, milady. You have friends and family to the north that may need you, if indeed there are ill tidings brewing."

"And what about you?" Enna asked, knowing the answer before the question was finished.

Adrik smiled at her. "It came to my attention very recently that I have spent my entire life running from things, out of fear of making difficult choices." He shot a quick look to Falken before continuing. "Regardless of how much I run, however, the fact remains that this, this title, these people, and right now this war, are all mine to bear. Morabendar needs a thane, and as such I must remain here to fulfill my duties." He placed his hand on Enna's shoulder, and looked to all in attendance, a smile on his face and a tear in his eye. "I have cherished my time with you all, truly, and I want you all to know that this is not the last time we shall cross paths. You've a friend in Thane Adrik Thornmallet," he said as he looked to Merida, "and a friend in all Morabendar."

Everyone was smiling then, yet there was no joy in the air, but rather a bittersweetness that hung heavy and low, engulfing all of the people present. There was silence for a long while, until it became so unbearable that someone had to speak. "So, what do we do now?" Erasmus asked, finally breaking the stillness.

"We head back to Deltharduin," Adrik replied, "and we bid one another farewell until we cross paths once more." The dwarf paused a moment, contemplating. "We shall set off in the morning.

Tonight, we feast, and celebrate our victory these past days." He patted his stomach thoughtfully. "Let us eat soon, too. By Othar's beard, I am positively famished."

Chapter 31

Enna, Erasmus, O'doc, and Falken spent their final days amid Morabendar relatively uneventfully, and in fine comfort. Merida remained at Otharbund with the Morabendine forces, and though fighting did not cease, the apparent display of arcane force that Enna had shown slowed and made hesitant further advancement from Ulbaryn, at least until word returned to the Ulbar commanders that the northern arcanist was no longer there, Enna surmised. Adrik threw himself actively into his role as thane immediately upon return, despite the protestations of his friends, and as such the group saw little of the dwarf in those final days before their departure. Nonetheless, none were surprised when the old dwarf personally escorted them to the snow-covered peaks above Deltharduin to see them safely off.

The bright sky overwhelmed the group, having been without it since their arrival to the Otharines, though the gray overcast clouds were indicative of how winter cast a shield about the sky and sun, making the transition somewhat more bareable. The great Khalenese owls, sedate for weeks due to runemagery, were all too anxious to be out in the open air, spreading and flapping their immense wings expectantly, even after Erasmus had charmed them back into obedience.

"I should like to know what sailing under the belly of one of those fine creatures is like one day," Adrik smiled brightly, admiring the owls. "Though I do concede, I would likely require some modifications to the steering mechanism to account for my..." he motioned to what remained of his left arm, "condition."

"I shall personally request it on behalf of his Lordship Thane Adrik of Morabendar," O'doc bowed with an exaggerated courtly flourish.

"Master O'doc, if ever I earnestly instill in you a need for such courtly rubbish, I must ask you to find what is left of my old arm and slap me with it!" Adrik chuckled, and the others laughed in kind, as the dwarf brought the halfling into as tight an embrace as he could manage with one arm. "I shall miss our verbal sparring, friend. Keep yourself, and everyone else, out of trouble."

Adrik turned then to Falken. "Adrik," the professor's eyes were cast down slightly. "I want to apologize for..."

The dwarf put up a hand to stop him. "In as brief a time as we have known one another, Professor," he said in Dwarfish, "you have managed to impart to me some of the best advice I have received in many years. I do not begrudge you in that, nor do I regret how I have chosen to hear it."

Falken smiled both in happiness and relief. "Thank you. Farewell, Adrik." He moved in to shake the dwarf's hand, only to have Adrik's thick hand pull him into a hug as well, which he reciprocated sincerely, if awkwardly.

Turning to Erasmus, Adrik looked up, a lopsided smirk on the half-elf's face. "I've not seen you smile like that for a good long while now," the dwarf noted.

"Lots more responsibilities lately than I'm used to, friend," Erasmus shrugged in response. "Easier to smile when you're carefree, you ought to know that."

"Erasmus Stonehand, that is no excuse," Adrik half-admonished in a fatherly tone, and smiled, "nor am I the best example by which to model responsibility."

"Recent events seem to argue otherwise," Erasmus countered. "And don't worry," he added, "'The Ballad of Thane Adrik' will make you seem quite the role model."

"I look forward to hearing it," Adrik grinned through his beard, and the two hugged warmly.

Finally, Adrik turned to Enna. The elf was smiling warmly at him, blinking back tears. "Now milady, I'll not have you shed any more tears on my account," he said, pulling her in close. "Especially lest you rain some manner of great arcane energy down upon us all as a result."

"I'm going to miss you, Adrik," Enna replied with a laugh as they hugged, unable to help it when a few tears streamed down her cheek.

"And I you, milady," the dwarf replied. "I shall regret not playing a greater role in your quest for self discovery." He stood back as they regarded one another. "Though I cannot offer thanks enough to all of you for aiding me in mine."

It was shortly thereafter that the group was airborne, the figure of Adrik waving farewell becoming no more than a speck that eventually disappeared into the peaks of the Otharine Mountains below.

Enna remained contemplative during their flight north, her mind alight with the many happenings that had not yet fully sunk into her mind. How had she cast the spell at Otharbund so easily, and with so few repercussions to herself? The moment replayed in her mind over and over, despite her best efforts to push it from her thoughts. She had killed thinking beings, not in self-defense, but wrath. Revisiting those feelings made her queasy, doubly so when she considered what her parents would have thought of the whole ordeal.

Her parents. Enna's stomach sank further at the thought of them. She had not so much as written two words to them in weeks, not that she would have known what to tell them, exactly. Regardless, she was certain that they would have been worried sick by now. The elf knew she had been worried about them since Erasmus and O'doc broke news of this impending war. The Summerlark farmstead and its occupants would not be of any interest to Lohvast, but their proximity to Rheth did give Enna pause, so much so that she nearly missed the others as their owls began to descend into the thick woods of Khalen Ridge. As the group got closer, however, a sharp odour cut through the air that worried the elf. Her fears were magnified as they descended further, and her eyes, able to pierce through the darkness of night with the aid of the dwarven amulet, caught the faintest remnants of smoke billowing up from an area just northeast of where they were about to land.

The group landed gently in the clearing from which they had taken flight all those weeks prior, and it became evident to Enna that she was not the only one who noticed that something was amiss. O'doc in particular, practically ripped himself from his harness, taking off in a sprint down one of the paths from the clearing. "There must have been a fire!" he cried out to the others as they tried to match his pace. He said nothing else, nor did anyone else as they moved as quickly as they could following the halfling down the snow-covered path, until at last they reached a large expanse, its width and breadth spotted with a number of large trees, their canopies now bare, though still stretching across the whole of the area above. Amid the trees were what looked like the remnants of housing that had been built into them. Rope bridges with singed ends hung impotently from thick boughs, while below all manner of wood, clay, and stone lay strewn chaotically about the ground, smoldering remains of brick, mortar, and carpentry. In the middle of it all was Odonwa Overhill, kneeling in the snow and angrily hammering one hand into the trunk of a tree.

O'doc cried out his sisters name and ran toward her, his friends trailing behind him. She appeared to not have heard him initially, uttering a string of curses that became more audible as the younger halfling approached. It was only when O'doc was within a few feet that Odonwa looked up, her eyes suddenly widening with surprise as she sprang to her feet and hugged her brother tightly.

"It's gone..." she said in a voice that was equal parts anger and despair. "I was out chopping firewood when I heard great thunderous crashes. I ran back as quick as I could..."

"Are mom and dad still...?"

"In Hallowspire, yes, thank Sheandre," Odonwa finished her brother's question as she stepped back, reaching into a pocket in her thick winter cloak, and producing a single piece of parchment. "But I found this stuck to one of the trees..."

O'doc took the page from his sister, the grave expression in her eyes putting his stomach in knots. Looking at the page, his face blanched.

"What is it?" Erasmus asked.

"It's a note in our aunt Caliope's handwriting." Odonwa answered, her eyes moving to each of the others as she spoke. "It looks like she was being dictated to, but I cannot for the life of me figure out by whom."

"Well, what does it say?" Falken asked, now evidently more distressed by the knowledge that his old friend was involved.

O'doc said nothing, instead simply shaking his head slowly as his eyes, full of pure fear, scanned the page.

Hello Lambkins,

I'm having your dear, sweet aunt write this, as you well know I was never the writer. I must say, old friend, you and yours did a fine job keeping your humble abode tucked away, so far from my reach, but things have changed recently. You see, I got myself a new lot in life recently, and some of the benefits are extraordinary, the remodeling job I did is a small taste of that.

Anyway, I'm back off to Lohvast, big things brewing out west, in case you've not heard. I'm taking your aunt along, as well. She and I have become quite close, and she's proving quite useful. Don't bother trying to follow and find us, because we both know I'm far to smart for you to succeed at that. Don't worry, though, Lambkins, I'll be back for a more personal visit soon.

Cheers, Lambkins,
Lannister.

Erasmus shook his head, a troubled look crossing his face. "It's Ravenclaw, isn't it?"

Odonwa's expression changed quickly as she looked back to O'doc, becoming one of angry suspicion. "You know who did this?!" the elder Overhill leaped at the younger, hands out as though she meant to strangle him. O'doc was quick to dodge his sister's lunge, and Falken moved in to easily subdue her, holding her by the shoulders as she swung her arms ineffectually at her brother.

"You rat!" she cried out. "I ought to strike you down with a bolt of lightning where you stand!"

"You think I wanted this to happen?!" The younger Overhill shouted back. "Why do you think I never came back home? So people like Lannister Ravenclaw wouldn't do this!" he motioned angrily to the smoldering remains of his childhood home.

"Serves you right, dealing with damned low-life filth!" she spat. "You ought to have stayed away."

"You're right." O'doc said soberly, all the fight gone from his voice. "I should have, but I had a friend who needed my help. This whole mess is my fault, and you have my word that I will deal with it personally."

Odonwa, having stopped thrashing, was released by Falken, and stormed up to her brother until they were face-to-face. She looked into O'doc's eyes a long while, a dower look on her face, until she nodded, satisfied. "You never could lie to me, Honeytongue," she said, her scowl and agitated tone running in contrast to her use of the younger halfling's nickname.

"I'll be damned, though, if I set you off by yourself to handle family business like this. I'm coming with you." The rest of the party looked to one another, each able to tell that the matter clearly was not up for discussion.

"You know you have my aid," Erasmus said, placing a hand on O'doc's shoulder.

"All of our aid," Enna corrected, with Falken nodding next to her.

O'doc smiled half-heartedly at the elf. "Enna, I can't ask you to help me in this. Our entire reason for setting out was to help you find out who you are..."

"There is quite a lot I still have to learn about myself," Enna interrupted, "but there is a lot that I already do know. I know I have good friends, who did not once hesitate to help me, I know that I am just as eager to help those friends when they need it, and I know that whatever mysteries are surrounding me won't change in the time it takes me to do so."

O'doc nodded, his smile brightening somewhat. "Well, it looks as though that's settled. Where do we begin?"

"Back in East Fellowdale, at my manor," Falken reasoned. "There's a chance we might find a clue there, some evidence from Caliope."

The rest nodded their assent, and promptly made off, O'doc casting one last look at what was left of his childhood home.

"We can rebuild it," Odonwa said, her voice quiet, her hand on her brother's shoulder. "The important thing now is that we focus on Aunt Caliope."

O'doc nodded, and slowly turned to walk away, painfully aware of the fact that he would never see his home again, not as he had before he left. The halfling had tried so hard for so many years to remove himself from his past, that he was taken aback by seeing it ripped so permanently away, which only amplified the pain of the loss all the more.

It took until late the next morning for the group to find their way back to East Fellowdale, in part due to the fact that all five eventually gave into their inevitable fatigue late in the night, and made camp against their own wishes, though their sleep was short and fretful. When the group finally made it to Falken's manor, their tired bodies and eyes almost could not register the fact that, as they entered, the study opposite the front door was not unoccupied. Rather, a slender elven woman lay in the room's plush chaise, her face hidden behind one of the professor's books, only barely taking note of the group as they entered.

"Welcome home, Professor," the elf said simply, otherwise disregarding the group as she flipped idly through the tome. "I tried to keep the place tidy while you were gone."

Falken stood agog a moment, but quickly shook the feeling, thinking this might somehow connect to Caliope's disappearance. "Who are you?" he asked as commandingly as he was able, as he subtly began to reach for the wand at his belt, noting the others were readying themselves similarly.

"Come now, Professor..." the elf purred, lowering the book to reveal a pair of large golden eyes. "Do you not recognize me?" She stood elegantly and bowed subtly to the group. "To be sure, I have met most of you already," she turned her eyes to Erasmus, who looked as though he had been punched square in the chest. "Some of you many, many years ago."

"Zarah?" the professor and the bard asked in unified disbelief.

Zarah kept her eyes on the half-elf, and smiled wryly. "Hello, Erasmus Stonehand. It has been a long time."

Epilogue

In her modest homestead in Hallowspire, not far from castle Rheth, Tessa Summerlark had seen her fair share of oddities. Some were inanimate curios dragged in by her husband Randis during his youthful days as a traveling merchant. Some were people of varying races and backgrounds, such as the young elf who lost her life, and in doing so gave Randis and Tessa their beloved Enna, or the half-elf, halfling, and dwarf who had agreed to see Enna through the trials and tribulations she had yet to come. Some were even as simple as letters, written to the Summerlarks by extraordinary people. Letters from rogue archmages delivered by the King's Guard, and most recently from dwarven thanes, dropped from on high by great eagles.

How and why Enna and her friends had wound up among the dwarves baffled, and initially angered the couple, notably Randis. "What in the hells kind of business has Enna got down in those mountains?" he would mutter, or, "Who talked her into this?" or occasionally, "Does that girl not even have the common courtesy to write letters to her own parents herself?" Most of it was blustering, of course.

At the end of the day, the occasional letters meant that their girl was safe out in the world, and that was all two parents could ask for.

"If I don't get a handwritten letter from that girl soon," Randis grumbled one day as Tessa perused the latest note brought to them, "written in her handwriting... Gods, you'd think the girl forgot all her manners by the time she was not two miles out that door..."

As if on cue, the door to which Randis pointed began to reverberate as three loud, purposeful knocks rang out from it. Randis looked to his wife, who shrugged unknowingly. Slowly, the old merchant-turned-farmer rose, and walked toward the door, grasping a heavy iron fire-poker from the kitchen hearth as he did.

Three more knocks rang out before Randis reached the door and opened it cautiously. A pair of heavily armored men stood on the outside of the door, flanking a smaller man in robes. Randis knew immediately upon sight that the men were not members of any Hallowspirian regiment, recognizing on the trio the distinct colours of the kingdom of Lohvast.

Tessa walked to the door to join her husband, but Randis placed his arm out defensively, stepping out front and in full view of the strange visitors. "Can I... help you, gentlemen?" he asked.

"We wish you no quarrel," the man in robes stated simply. "However, we have come to inform you that, by order of Queen Merrian Arkalis, this property has been deemed strategically important to Lohvast. We must ask that you vacate the premises within the next two days."

In her modest homestead in Hallowspire, not far from castle Rheth, Tessa Summerlark had seen her fair share of oddities, but this was wholly unexpected.

About the Author

Brandon Draga was born in 1986, just outside Toronto, Ontario. His love of all things fantasy began at an early age with games like *The Legend of Zelda*, *Heroquest*, and *Dungeons and Dragons*. This affinity for the arcane and archaic led to his studying history in university from 2005 to 2011. In late 2012, he began writing a D&D campaign setting that would lay the groundwork for the world of the Four Kingdoms. Brandon still lives just outside Toronto, and when he is not writing enjoys skateboarding, playing guitar, and playing tabletop games.

Made in the USA
Charleston, SC
29 October 2014